Prai

M000219754

"A good fun read ..."

— NINJA LIBRARIAN

"Claire Logan spins a tale that keeps you interested and wanting to read more."

— MY READING JOURNEYS

"All the characters are well developed, and the story is delightful."

— BARONESS BOOK TROVE

"... my favorite thing about this novel is the characters, especially Hector and Pamela. My second favorite is that the action is fast-paced, so you have have to be on your toes at times when trying to figure out the killer yourself."

— MELISSA WILLIAMS

"I recommend this book to cozy mystery readers that enjoy the look and feel and flavor of Prohibition Chicago."

— KAREN SIDDALL

For those of you who are starting over.

The Vanishing Valet!

The Myriad Mysteries #2

Claire Logan

1

A blue sky over Lake Michigan with just a few wisps of cloud, the buildings on Chicago's Lake Shore Drive clear and glittering in the distance.

The sails on the spacious yacht barely fluttered.

Mrs. Pamela Jackson reclined on a chaise lounge, now in a patch of half-shade cast by a sail, browsing a fashion magazine. She took a drag of her cigarette. Her black toy poodle Bessie nestled beside her, eyes closed.

Mrs. Jackson wore a bathing suit with a skirt which reached to her mid-thigh, covered with a sheer long-sleeved robe, which when she stood up grazed the floor. The whole outfit felt quite daring, but everyone she'd met assured her that here, it was entirely proper.

Her right arm held a four inch wide gauze bandage on the inside of her elbow. She rubbed at the skin beside it, which itched a bit.

Fashion didn't interest her too terribly much. But she'd just found something astonishing.

A full-page article lay before her bearing the photo of a young man with pale skin and straight black hair. He wore the tall white hat and high-collar jacket of a master Chef. The headline:

Prodigy Revitalizes Chicago Cuisine

Mrs. Jackson smiled fondly at the photo. Bringing the magazine closer, she began to read.

Footsteps approached from behind. Bessie sprang up, barking.

Mrs. Jackson petted little Bessie. "Hush, dear."

Although Bessie quieted, a suspicious gleam remained in her eye.

Mr and Mrs. Neuberg approached: brown hair, slightly tanned, brown eyes. With the exception of Mr. Neuberg's red linen vest and tan deck shoes, the pair were entirely dressed in white. They held drinks, relaxing into the chairs across the table. Mr. Neuberg said, "Can I get you anything?"

Mrs. Jackson lay the magazine on the small, low rectangular wooden table beside her, then gestured to her half-full glass of lemonade, the ice mostly melted. "No need, thank you."

Mrs. Neuberg said, "Where are the boys?"

Mrs. Jackson felt amused. Her Mr. Jackson was over thirty, and even Mrs. Neuberg's son George was in his middle twenties. Hardly boys. "I checked on them an hour ago. Exhausted, poor dears."

Mr. Neuberg chuckled. "Fishing will do that to you. Fresh air, vigorous exertion. The battle for mastery of the beast. It's good for them. Young men need to be out more often, I say. Back in my day we didn't stay indoors all the time like they do now."

A deep voice said, "Is that so?"

Mr. Hector Jackson emerged onto the deck. Tall, very dark-skinned, he wore dark round spectacles he called "sun-glasses" (an affectation certain celebrities had taken up of late), a navy and white striped shirt, and navy Bermuda shorts (with deck shoes to match). He beamed at them all. "I suppose you're right."

Mr. Jackson knelt beside her and took her hand, kissing her cheek. "Have you been enjoying yourself?"

"Ever so much." Mrs. Jackson had always enjoyed sailing, and the day was excellent.

Bessie barked, ears up and tail wagging.

Mr. Jackson took the little dog into his arms and stood, ruffling her curly black hair. "And how do you like this lake today? Hmm?"

A chuckle came from below, and George Neuberg emerged onto the deck. Not nearly so tall as Mr. Jackson, George dressed in a white shirt and tan khaki trousers. His face held a pink tinge, perhaps from spending all day in the sun.

A chorus of "George!" came forth.

Mr. Jackson took off his dark spectacles, folded them, and slid them into his shirt pocket.

George's mother went to hug her son. "Did you boys rest well?"

George grinned, his cheeks reddening. "I'd say so." He surveyed the sparkling lake around them. "I feel quite refreshed."

"Come join us," his father said. "We were napping up front and just got here."

Mrs. Jackson held out her hand, feeling a great fondness for the young man. "Dear George."

At that, George took her hand and kissed her cheek as well. Then he knelt beside her, still holding her hand, and spoke earnestly. "My dear Mrs. Jackson. I hope you weren't feeling abandoned."

Mrs. Jackson laughed. "With such a glorious view? Never. And I had Bessie for company the entire time." The little dog seemed to like boats, which was fortunate, given the amount of time they'd spent aboard them over the past few months.

Mr. Neuberg said, "What do you think? About time to start dinner?"

George chuckled. "That means he's hungry."

"Come, Pamela, dear," Mrs. Neuberg said to Mrs. Jackson. "Let's get everything set up."

Mrs. Jackson looked up at Mr. Jackson. "That last fish you caught was splendid." She glanced at Bessie, who still lay in his arms, little ears perking up at the attention. "I'll bet there's a fine slice waiting for you!"

The two women descended to the galley and began gathering the pale green Lusterware dishes and silver flatware onto a tray.

It took Mrs. Neuberg a while to speak. "We're very grateful for your attentions to our son."

Ah. As she'd guessed. "Such a dear friend. He and Mr. Jackson have so very much in common."

"And you?"

"Me? We both like to sail, although I've much to learn." She shrugged. "I think your son's very sweet." She patted the older woman's hand. "He worries he's taking too much of Mr. Jackson's time, us newly married and all. But he forgets we've spent the past few months in close proximity!"

Mrs. Neuberg chuckled. "I do see your point."

Mrs. Jackson smiled to herself. "I'm grateful your son and my Mr. Jackson have become friends."

The yacht was grand: an oiled wooden deck large enough for parties, with several bedrooms and a spacious galley below. But on this day, Mr. Neuberg grilled fish upon a small charcoal stove bolted to the deck. The couple sat under an umbrella, its pole running through the center of a fine table made of white wire.

Mrs. Jackson sat to Mr. Jackson's right; little Bessie lay nestled on the deck between them. After bustling about with salad and sliced fruit, Mrs. Neuberg sat beside Mrs. Jackson.

Mr. Neuberg brought the fish and sat next to his wife, that is to say, directly across from Mr. Jackson.

Mrs. Jackson set a slice of fish on a saucer and tested the temperature before giving Bessie her promised prize.

The little dog danced about, tail wagging, as she set upon her meal.

"Good girl," Mrs. Jackson said, smoothing Bessie's soft black curls. When Mrs. Jackson returned to her plate, it had been filled!

A glimpse at Mr. Jackson's face told the story. "Thank you!"

He leaned over with a smile to kiss her cheek. "Think nothing of it."

As everyone ate, Mrs. Neuberg said, "Mr. Jackson, you're quite the good influence on my George! Beds made, sheets changed and everything!" She sounded astonished, and a bit embarrassed. "I could've done all that for you."

Mr. Jackson laughed, nudging George, who sat to his left. "So you're a slovenly fellow, are you? We'll have to fix that!"

George grimaced, appearing embarrassed.

Mr. Jackson turned to George's mother. "No trouble at all. I believe in being a good guest."

George's mother sounded impressed. "You've been well-taught!"

Mr. Neuberg said, "What are your plans?"

Mr. Jackson let go of her hand, took up his plate, and leaned back, holding his plate at the level of his heart. He gestured with his fork as he spoke. "We don't need to rush off. Unless some disaster occurs, we should be in Chicago for as long as we like."

Mrs. Neuberg leaned forward. "Won't you come to stay with us? It'd be no trouble at all."

Mr. Jackson said, "Certainly not! We've imposed upon your hospitality long enough."

This was the third time Mrs. Neuberg had asked this. Mrs. Jackson said, "We've enjoyed our time here with you ever so much."

Mr. Jackson glanced over at her. "Indeed we have! And we'd love to sail more in the future."

Having said what she wished, Mrs. Jackson decided to completely let go of the discussion. "I would enjoy that." She set her fork down, then gazed over the water, letting the air calm her, and spoke with sincerity. "I truly do love boats."

George said, "Aww, come on, Ma. Stop badgering them. I'm scheduled in for the whole week! And I'm sure they have their own plans."

Mr. Neuberg glanced at his wife, who seemed mollified at her son's words. "Very well. Will you stay at the Myriad, then?"

Mr. Jackson said, "Of course. They have our suite held for us. I called from the station to let them know we were in town."

Mrs. Neuberg said, "I'm surprised you'd go back!"

Mr. Jackson laughed, setting his plate and fork on the table. "It really was a misunderstanding all round."

"I suppose ..." Mrs. Neuberg didn't seem convinced.

"In any case," Mr. Jackson continued, "we simply must visit our friends there as well!" His face changed, as if he'd come into an idea. "Why don't you meet us one night for dinner? I hear this new Chef is excellent."

That, of course, reminded Mrs. Jackson of the article. The thought of seeing her young friend after so many years felt thrilling.

"Oh," Mrs. Neuberg said, "I'd like that. I read about him in the paper."

"Then it's settled," Mr. Jackson said. "Telephone when you decide on a date — we'll make a reservation."

Mrs. Neuberg said, "Why not next Monday? George will be off, and we can spend as long as we like."

George didn't seem entirely pleased with eating dinner on his day off at his own place of employment, but he said nothing.

"I'll make all the arrangements," Mr. Jackson said.

Mr. Neuberg stood. "It's getting late."

Bessie leapt to her feet, barking until Mrs. Jackson took the little dog onto her lap.

George checked his watch, then tapped it. "I think it's stopped."

Mr. Neuberg began to gather the plates. Mrs. Neuberg collected the glasses. "Isn't it past time for a new watch, dear?"

George shrugged. "I like this one." He examined the brown leather band. "Although I suppose it is getting a bit ratty."

Mrs. Neuberg said, "But you've had it fixed three times now."

Then Mr. Neuberg said, "George, take us back to shore, if you will."

"Sure, Dad." George headed for the anchor.

Mrs. Jackson glanced at Bessie, then at Mr. Neuberg's retreating back, then at Mr. Jackson. "Something about him startles her."

Mr. Jackson ruffled the little dog's hair. "But you are an excellent little alarm, though, aren't you?"

Bessie wagged her tail, eyes bright.

This amused Mrs. Jackson no end. "Did you enjoy your weekend?"

Mr. Jackson put an arm around her then gently kissed her cheek. "I most certainly did. And you?"

She considered this. "I did. The weekend has been most pleasant."

Mr. Jackson rested his head on hers, face turned toward the approaching skyline of Chicago. "I wonder what's been going on at our dear old Myriad Hotel."

***

After docking, everyone changed into clothes suitable for the street, then stowed the umbrella and furniture. The Neubergs insisted on driving Mr. Jackson and his wife to the Hotel.

By the time they arrived, darkness had completely fallen. The sidewalks were busy: people going to and fro, in and out of the hotel. Bright electric bulbs lit the underside of the wide overhang which sheltered their guests. Cars lined up in the circle drive in front of the Hotel as people left for their evening entertainments.

Mr. Neuberg parked his car alongside the others. As everyone got out of the car and came round to the sidewalk, Mr. Jackson clipped on Bessie's black leather leash, and set her on the ground. Then he turned to the Neubergs. "Thank you so much for your hospitality."

George's mother hugged them both. George shook hands with Mr. Jackson, kissed Mrs. Jackson on the cheek, then said, "See you tomorrow." Then George and his mother returned to the car.

Mr. Jackson shook hands with Mr. Neuberg. "See you next Monday then?"

Mr. Neuberg grinned. "Wouldn't miss it. You two have a good evening!"

A red-haired valet got into the car in front of them and drove off.

Mr. Neuberg unlocked the car's trunk.

A brown-haired bellhop with round spectacles took the couple's bags. The man's nametag, white and ringed in brass with dark lettering said: Melvin. "Need someone to park you?"

Mr. Neuberg waved him away. "Just dropping off."

"Very good, sir." Melvin turned to the couple. "Right this way, please."

Mr. Jackson took his wife's arm and started towards the doorway.

Bessie, however, began pulling to the left.

2

Mr. Jackson tugged her back towards them. "Come on, girl."

His wife said, "Is something wrong?"

The bellhop stood at the heavy glass outer door with their bags, waiting.

Grateful he'd put the leash on, Mr. Jackson picked Bessie up, tucking the little dog under his left arm. It would've been a nightmare if she'd gotten loose here in the open street. "I'd wager someone dropped a bit of food." He grinned at Mrs. Jackson, offering her his right arm. "Let's get her settled."

What a chase she'd led them on, that last day aboard the steamer! They'd neglected to apply her leash, thinking Bessie would stay close by, but off she went. He never realized there were so many dogs on that ship until then.

The couple moved past the doormen and into the wide lobby, which was every bit as spectacular as he recalled: a tall fine fountain in the center, surrounded by tan marble floors and rosewood trimmed with brass. They followed the bellhop through the crowd to the front desk, and this time, the Head Clerk stood there.

Mr. Lee Francis, a blond man in his early twenties, broke into smiles when he saw them. "Welcome back! I'd hoped to see you before I left for the day."

Mr. Jackson shook hands with the man. "So good to see you. I hope you and your family are well?"

"Quite." He fumbled with his wallet, drawing out a small photo of a newborn baby. "My son."

Mrs. Jackson peered at the photo. "He's lovely!"

"Admirable chap," Mr. Jackson said, and meant it. "How old is he now?"

"One month tomorrow," Mr. Francis said, beaming.

"My most sincere congratulations," said Mr. Jackson. "Glad you're here! I quite thought we'd miss seeing you. Working late?"

"One of our men fell sick and went home early." He shook his head with a wry grin. "The bad part about being Head Clerk is you end up filling in."

Mr. Jackson chuckled. "Quite."

Mr. Francis put the photo away. "Let's see to your rooms." He thumbed through a small file. "Here you are! Suite 3205, as requested." He peered at the card, which had yellow paper attached with a clip. "Looks like Effie spilled something: she's still cleaning it." He glanced aside, then back. "Would you wait while I call up?" Mr. Francis moved down the long front desk to the phone.

***

Mrs. Jackson glanced down beside her: their bags sat neatly upon the floor by her feet.

It felt good to be back. To see familiar faces again.

The desk clerk, who her Mr. Jackson seemed to know well, stood a ways off, using the telephone.

As she waited, Mrs. Jackson's eyes strayed over the area behind the front desk. A door, which from previous experience went to a hallway beyond, then a whole array of keys, each in their own wooden square, fobs dangling. On the rosewood counter in front of her and to the right sat a number of brochures for the Hotel.

The front read:

Live In Luxury!

A photograph of the Myriad Hotel had been taken from so far back that its cobblestone alleyways could be seen on either side. She wondered: since the building faced Lake Shore Drive, how did he get this shot? Perhaps a stand of some sort out on the shore? That must have taken some doing.

It truly was a splendid photograph, although the photographer would have had to take the image from a boat to display the Hotel's full height. The day would have to be quite calm, she thought. Or could you take a photograph from an aeroplane?

She shook her head, amused at herself, and opened the brochure.

> The fabulous Myriad Hotel has been among the best in fine living and dining in Chicago since its opening in 1897. Whether visiting for a day or a year, the Myriad has everything you'll need.

The desk clerk said, "The room's ready for you now. She was just letting the carpet air out." He handed the suite keys to Mr. Jackson and a small brown paper sack to her. "Some chopped meat from dinner for your dog. I had Effie lay a saucer on your dresser."

Bessie's ears went up. She began struggling in Mr. Jackson's arms, tail wagging, her nose going towards the paper sack.

Mrs. Jackson felt touched at his thoughtfulness. "That's very kind of you!

The clerk smiled. "Enjoy your stay!"

A different bellhop came up and took their bags. Mrs. Jackson followed him and Mr. Jackson to their suite's parlor, which smelled faintly of soap. Two doors, one on each side, led to the bedrooms, each having its own door to the hallway. The three rooms each had their own balcony. A magnificent view of the lake faced them through plate windows.

Mr. Jackson pointed to the left door. "Those bags go in her room there." Then he pointed to the right door. "Mine go there."

The man hesitated just an instant, then brought everything to where directed.

Once the bellhop left, Mr. Jackson unclipped Bessie's leash and set her on the floor, where she set to smelling the thick black carpeting around her, then everything in the suite. He gestured for the small paper sack. "I'll set that out for her."

Mrs. Jackson handed the sack over and gazed around the parlor. The room was much as it had been when they left it: painted white, furnished in rosewood, with brass trim and cobalt blue cushions.

Mr. Jackson had disappeared into her bedroom; Mrs. Jackson trailed after him.

Her bags had been set neatly at the foot of her large bed, which was made up in black and white. A clink of a saucer being set on tile and the crinkle of a paper bag emerged from the bathroom. Bessie rushed past, all a rattling of little claws on little paws.

Mr. Jackson appeared from her bathroom. He chuckled, glancing behind him. "Guess she's hungry after all."

Mrs. Jackson let out a breath, feeling as if she were home. "I enjoyed sailing, but I'm glad to be here." She smiled at him, and he blushed, giving her a shy smile in return. Going to him, she cradled his face in her hands. "I really am happy you had a good time."

Mr. Jackson wrapped his arms around her waist. "My dear girl, the sight of you in that bathing suit has tormented me all weekend. I'm well glad to be alone with you at last."

3

Mrs. Jackson woke lazily, the sky outside the glass doors to her balcony a clear blue. She smiled at the dear sleeping face of the man she'd come to trust and admire these past months since their marriage.

Half-lit by the morning sun streaming onto his cheek, he reminded her of another man who'd loved her so deeply, yet now lay dead.

None of that will bring anything other than grief and trouble, Mr. Jackson had said once.

But memories weren't so easy to forget.

Perhaps if I focus on today, she thought, I might find some peace. She took a deep breath and let it out, relaxing into her pillow as she gazed about her room.

The door to the parlor stood open, as did the one to Mr. Jackson's room beyond. This amused her: they'd completely forgotten to close them.

A hissing noise came forth.

She sat up. In place of the usual white painted radiator, a metal one — bronze, or perhaps brass — stood there, shaped like golden flames!

Mr. Jackson said sleepily, "Hmm? What is it?"

She pointed. "An addition to our rooms."

Bessie leapt onto the bed, clambering back and forth over them.

Mrs. Jackson smoothed her little dog's hair. "Very well, Miss Bessie, I'll serve your breakfast."

Mr. Jackson chuckled, stretching out on the bed. "Who owns who, I wonder."

Mrs. Jackson retrieved her day bag. They'd bought a package of dog biscuits outside the station on the way into town. Mrs. Jackson put a handful into Bessie's little green ceramic bowl, which Bessie set to with enthusiasm.

A knock came at Mr. Jackson's door.

Mr. Jackson said, "Is it that late already?" He got up, putting on his trousers. "The clerk must have called for Mr. Vienna last night."

Mr. Norman Vienna was Mr. Jackson's hired manservant — or valet, as they called them here. They used the same word as for those men who parked the automobiles, yet their duties were completely different.

Mrs. Jackson found this amusing. "Ah. Then Mrs. Knight won't be far behind." She folded up the package of dog biscuits and put it aside. "You go on. I'll call for someone to walk our Queen Bess."

Chuckling, Mr. Jackson left for his room.

Mrs. Jackson put on a blue and white striped robe (courtesy of the Hotel) and went to the telephone. She'd gotten quite used to having a telephone in her room since she and Mr. Jackson first arrived here. A remarkable and useful tool indeed!

The veterinarian seemed thrilled that they'd returned. "My boys will be so excited. I'll send one up right away."

***

When Mr. Jackson answered the knock at his door, a young man he didn't recognize stood there. Early twenties, brown eyes, pale freckled skin and straight brown hair, he stood a full head shorter. The man wore a tweed cap, white shirt, brown tweed vest, brown trousers, and no gloves. "Good morning," Mr. Jackson said. "May I help you?"

The man doffed his cap, holding out a hand. "Stanley Raymond, sir, at your service. From the Howell-Green Procurement Agency. I'm to be your valet."

Mr. Jackson peered at the man, feeling foggy.

Mr. Raymond drew back a bit, hand still extended. "You did call for a manservant, did you not?"

"Oh," Mr. Jackson's confusion lifted. "Yes, of course!" He shook the man's hand. But then he felt concerned. "Has something happened to Mr. Vienna?"

"Not at all, sir," Mr. Raymond said. "His current assignment has gone longer than planned, that's all. I'm here to fill in."

Then Mr. Jackson remembered his manners and opened the door wide. "By all means, come in!" As the man came past, Mr. Jackson felt chagrined. "Forgive my rudeness: I've only just awakened."

Mr. Raymond glanced at the immaculate bed, the set of still-packed bags neatly placed upon it. "Think nothing of it, sir."

The sound of Bessie's feet came from the other room.

"My wife and I arrived last night," Mr. Jackson said, then felt foolish.

The man grinned. "No need to explain, sir. I'll get your things put away once I've run your bath." He went to the bathroom, and there came forth the sound of running water. "It should be ready in a few minutes, sir." He surveyed the room and Mr. Jackson's face. "Do you have special plans for the day?"

Mr. Jackson shook his head. "We might go walking, I suppose. But no, nothing special."

"Very good." He went to the bathroom and turned off the water. "Come now, sir, let's get you undressed."

"Mr. Vienna always wore gloves. Is there a reason you don't?"

Mr. Raymond grinned, holding out his hands. "I'm an odd size. Large gloves are too big and mediums are too small."

"Not even in winter?"

The new valet chuckled. "Mittens do fine outside. But at work?" He shrugged. "I just wash my hands."

And so he did, before and after each of his duties.

Mr. Jackson didn't know why he felt unsettled. The man seemed perfectly capable. His bath was just the right temperature. His shave was perfect.

This comes from waking so late, Mr. Jackson thought, and being startled awake at that.

As his tie was being straightened, Mr. Jackson noticed the valet's tie clasp: silvery metal with room for three gems. But only two stood there, both a deep murky red. "You're missing a gemstone."

Mr. Raymond looked down, face alarmed. "Oh, no." He began to peer around at the floor.

Mr. Jackson began looking as well. "Is the stone valuable?"

That sent the man into some thought. "I'm not rightly sure. But my grandfather gave me that clip before he died, and I'd hate to lose it."

"This sounds serious," Mr. Jackson said. "I'll leave a note for the maids."

Relief spread over the young valet's face. "Thank you, sir. My sister's the maid for this floor; she'll surely recognize it."

***

While Mr. Jackson spoke with his valet, Mrs. Jackson answered a knock on her door; Bessie followed. A boy of ten stood there.

His face burst into a smile. "Bessie!"

Bessie seemed just as excited to see him.

Amused, Mrs. Jackson knelt to clip Bessie's leash on (with some difficulty for all of Bessie's dancing about) then handed the leash to the boy.

As Bessie dragged the veterinarian's son down the hall, up the hall came Mrs. Octavia Knight.

Mrs. Knight was perhaps forty, a lady's maid for hire. She seemed ever so pleased to see Mrs. Jackson again, especially without her sling. Mrs. Knight helped Mrs. Jackson out of her robe. "How's your arm?"

"Very well," Mrs. Jackson said. "Don't mind the bandage; everything's perfectly healed. It's to protect my arm from the sun, so the scar fades instead of browning."

After undoing the bandage, Mrs. Knight examined the scar. "What a difference! You can hardly tell anything's been done!" She glanced at the pile of bags, which lay in a disorderly mound upon the floor. "Let's get you in your bath, then I'll take care of these."

The mound of bags, the disheveled bed, and all it implied set Mrs. Jackson's cheeks to burning. "Thank you," she finally said. "Choose out the long-sleeved dress, then we won't need the bandage."

"That would save time." Mrs. Knight moved past to turn on the bath. Then she glanced back over her shoulder. "Did they send up the hotplate for your tonic? I can get that started if you like."

"No need," Mrs. Jackson said. "When I was at the specialist surgeon's, they did tests on my blood! To see one's own blood in a vial is the most peculiar feeling."

Mrs. Knight sat on the edge of the tub, her eyes widening. "I imagine."

"But the doctor said everything's in order! I won't need the tonic for now. I'm to return in a year for a recheck, but," she shrugged, "it seems I'm recovered!"

Mrs. Knight beamed. "I'm so very happy for you."

It still felt odd not to take her tonic every day. Mrs. Jackson took a deep breath. It felt like a new chance.

"I'll have them take the hotplate away, then," was all Mrs. Knight said on the subject. Mrs. Knight clearly wished to ask why she'd needed the tonic in the first place, but had never said a word, for which Mrs. Jackson felt grateful.

***

After the couple had been dressed, Mr. Jackson led his wife down to breakfast. The long dining room was almost at capacity, waiters and maids coming and going around large round tables holding people in various stages of their meals. An attractive young man played upon the grand piano on its dais in the midst of the room, his soft music filling the air.

Mr. Jackson spied George across the room hard at work, dressed in his waiter's uniform. Their eyes met; George gave him a quick smile and a nod.

Mr. Jackson smiled fondly at him. Could they possibly sneak in one more boating trip before the cold weather hit?

The dowager Duchess Cordelia Stayman sat at one of the many large round tables, that particular one half full. Glancing up, she wiped her mouth then hurried over, the beads on her pale tan morning gown rattling. "Oh, my dear Mrs. Jackson! And Mr. Jackson! I have been counting the days!" She took each of their arms in hers, escorting them back to her table. "You must sit with me and tell me everything of your journey!"

The other guests at her table smiled to themselves.

Several seats around the dowager were empty. Mr. Jackson gestured for his wife to sit next to the dowager, then sat to the right of his wife. "I hope you're well?"

The dowager blushed. "Quite well, sir. And you?"

"Got in late last night."

A waiter came up. His name-tag said: Will. "Care for some drinks, sir?"

"Ah, yes," Mr. Jackson said. "Coffee for me, heavy cream, no sugar." He turned to his wife. "Tea?"

"Yes, I'll have tea, thank you."

A woman across the table said, "It was nice meeting you, ma'am. We're off to the station." She and several of the guests rose, so Mr. Jackson did too.

"Goodbye," the dowager said, waving to them as they left. Then she turned to the couple. "Such lovely people. Only stayed overnight, more's the pity." Her manner became enthusiastic. "Now you must positively tell me about your trip! How is your arm? Did you see the surgeon?

As a busboy moved in to clear the remaining plates across the table, Mr. Jackson resumed his seat.

Mrs. Jackson said, "I did!" She held out her right arm, bending and straightening in under its long sleeve. "Good as new!"

Duchess Cordelia seemed to relax. "I'm so glad. I've worried this entire time."

"That's very kind of you," Mr. Jackson said. "But there was no need to fret." He rested an arm around his wife's shoulders. "I've taken good care of her."

His wife nodded, her deep blue eyes twinkling. "He has! Oh, you should see our little villa in Tuscany. It's gorgeous. We would love to have you come visit. And the view!"

He felt glad the two continued their chatter, as he had no words. The fact that she said "our villa" instead of "his villa" moved him no end.

She's finally accepted me.

Something in the trip over on the steamer to Europe had calmed the nights of weeping in his arms for the husband and little son she'd so suddenly lost. For many nights in Tuscany, though, she lay beside him, eyes open, unmoving.

It was only on the long days back that she seemed to truly recover from her ordeal. He'd find her on deck, staring out over the water hat in hand, heedless of the wind or rain. But she'd turn to him and smile, and all would be right again.

"Your coffee, sir," the waiter said.

Yet she'd never spoken about what happened.

As he took his arm from around his wife's shoulders, she turned to him. "You're awfully quiet."

Mr. Jackson smiled at her. "So I am." Then he said to the dowager, "What news?"

Duchess Cordelia had lived at the Myriad Hotel for over three years, and was — at least in her own mind — the absolute expert on the goings-on there.

"Oh, the new Chef is simply marvelous," Duchess Cordelia said, beaming.

A passing waiter smiled at her, then continued on.

Duchess Cordelia fanned herself. "And so good looking, too!"

Out of the corner of his eye, Mr. Jackson saw his wife give a bemused smile. He said, "I'd heard he's done well, but —"

"You have no idea," Duchess Cordelia said. "Simply magnificent!"

Seeing their waiter approach, Mr. Jackson said, "Then I'm excited to see breakfast!"

Will chuckled as he put down the plates. "Good timing then, sir."

Mr. Jackson said, "Indeed!" He cut off a small piece and took a bite: Eggs Mornay, the thick white cheese sauce lightly spiced. "Delicious!"

Mrs. Jackson, mouth full, nodded. "Mm-hmm."

As they ate, Duchess Cordelia spoke at length about some scandal involving a young — unmarried — couple found after hours in the back of the library. It was most amusing, although their parents must have found it less so. Then the dowager said, "You simply must see the new collection. They have a whole set of historicals!"

Mr. Jackson wiped his mouth. "We have plenty of time. I don't plan to leave this hotel ever again, if I can manage it." While he enjoyed their travels, he hadn't realized how much he missed George until their reunion.

Duchess Cordelia said, "And you simply must come tonight after dinner and play dominoes."

Mrs. Jackson shrugged. "I've never played."

At the same time, Mr. Jackson said, "Really? Are you certain? We'd hate to intrude."

"You'd be the guests of honor!" Her smile slipped. "Even though my poor Albert's not with us anymore, he insisted we keep up the game." After a moment, her enthusiasm returned. "Please join us. I moved it to Tuesday nights: it's the slowest day, so the most people can participate. We all play — the maids, the waiters, anyone who wishes. I'm certain he'd want you there."

Mr. Jackson nodded, feeling a twinge of sadness. He missed Albert as well. "Then we'll be happy to attend."

***

Mrs. Jackson saw the sadness in his eyes, and patted his hand. He'd formed a bond with the dowager's husband the last time they'd been here.

A pity, how that all turned out.

She turned back to the old woman. "Do they ride bicycles here?"

Duchess Cordelia seemed surprised. "Of course! Although I haven't ridden in some time. I used to love it as a child." She drew back, hand to her chin. "They say you never forget!"

Mrs. Jackson chuckled. "Well, I have learned how. My Mr. Jackson here taught me." She reached beside her to squeeze his hand. "Taught me to swim as well." Where she'd come from, only men and boys actually went full into the water.

Duchess Cordelia gasped. "You never learned to swim? Or ride a bicycle? Well, my dear, it seems your education is lacking! What else do you not know?"

Mr. Jackson laughed. "Now, my Lady, how would she know what she didn't know?"

Mrs. Jackson thought that insight quite amusing.

Duchess Cordelia gained a new energy. "Then I shall make your education a project —"

At that, Mrs. Jackson laughed. A project!

"— because no young woman should go without experiencing all the world has to offer! You don't want to get to be my age and regret missing out."

"She does have a point," Mr. Jackson said.

Duchess Cordelia beamed. "I shall begin by teaching you dominoes!"

Mrs. Jackson found that most amusing.

Will hovered past Mr. Jackson. "May I take your plates, sir?"

He turned to the man. "Why yes." Then he glanced at them. "I think we're done here, are we not?"

Mrs. Jackson nodded, then spoke to the waiter. "When does your Chef arrive? We'd like to meet him."

"He's been here all morning, ma'am. You've caught us at a busy time, what with the tourists and all." He glanced aside, then back. "And we're a bit short-staffed this week."

"We don't wish to intrude," Mrs. Jackson said. "When would be the best time to greet him?"

"The staff sits for dinner at 7. We do the cooking to give him a rest. If you come by at, say, 6:30, he should be available."

Mrs. Jackson felt excited. "Wonderful!" Then she held up her hand. "Don't tell him we're here, if you would. I'd like it to be a surprise."

"Won't hear of it from me."

Duchess Cordelia's eyes were wide. "You know him, then?"

Mrs. Jackson smiled to herself. "You might say that."

After breakfast, Duchess Cordelia insisted they tour the library, so the couple did. Mrs. Jackson and the dowager moved to the velvet-bound rosewood seats and relaxed into them.

Mr. Jackson didn't join them. "I must fetch Bessie."

Mrs. Jackson smiled up at him fondly. He'd certainly warmed to her little dog since they'd found the poor thing starving outside the hotel. She took his hand. "Thank you."

"Of course. We don't want our 'Queen Bess' to overstay her welcome!" He winked at her, then left.

A laugh burst from Duchess Cordelia: heads turned towards them. She said more quietly, "Queen Bess?"

"Just something I made up this morning."

"It does fit." Then she sat up straighter. "Now you must tell me about your trip!"

Mrs. Jackson chuckled. "Have I not been telling you this entire morning? Very well. These cities are a marvel! So many sights, the people!" Having spent her entire life before her marriage to Mr. Jackson in one backwater town, she still felt astonished at it all. "We met with the specialist surgeon, but apparently the man is quite in demand — it took almost a month to have the surgery."

She extended and bent her right arm, going over it with her left hand. "Then we took a steamer ship to Tuscany. I've never seen so much water in my life!"

Duchess Cordelia nodded. "I remember our travels, Albert and I — before we came here."

From her face, Mrs. Jackson guessed the memory was now bittersweet. She put a hand on the dowager's.

But the old woman's face brightened. "It was a good time." She pulled her hand back, straightened her clothes, dusted off her dress. "Don't mind me; I just wish he were here."

Mrs. Jackson nodded. Wishing to change the subject for Duchess Cordelia's sake, she continued: "I was almost well when we got to Tuscany. Which was a good thing!" She smiled to herself, recalling their time in the sun. "But after a while, we both felt ready to return."

"I'm glad you did." She reached out to rest her hand on Mrs. Jackson's. "I missed you both terribly."

Mrs. Jackson felt moved at this, turning to put her other hand on top of Duchess Cordelia's. "I've missed you, too."

They sat together, both having endured and lost so much, yet even now able to find comfort in friendship and joy in a pleasure shared.

Mrs. Jackson said finally, "Which of those new books do you think I should read first?"

"Well, since you like Emerson, perhaps Thoreau?"

Mr. Jackson and Bessie approached then. He sat across the low round table from them, resting Bessie on his lap, where she settled in. "Are you two enjoying yourselves?"

"Let me get that book for you." Duchess Cordelia left for the stacks.

"We are," Mrs. Jackson said. "Did our girl receive a good report?"

Bessie's eyes were closed.

Mr. Jackson chuckled, smoothing the little dog's hair. "I think those boys tired her out." The veterinarian had several boys ranging from ten to sixteen, who adored their "little Bessie."

"Here you are," the dowager said, book in hand. "I've heard good things about this one."

Mrs. Jackson took the copy of *Walden, Or Life in the Woods* from Duchess Cordelia. The cover looked a bit dreary, so she set it in the space between herself and the armrest. "I'll check it out to read in my rooms."

Mr. Jackson said, "Where shall we have luncheon?"

Mrs. Jackson chuckled. "Do you need to ask? We simply must visit Miss Goldie Jean!"

The dowager clapped her hands. "Splendid!"

Several of the other library patrons glanced over.

Duchess Cordelia lowered her voice, cheeks coloring. "You will completely enjoy it. She's gotten ever so much commerce, she needs to expand."

Mrs. Jackson felt surprised: the shop had barely opened. "Already?"

"Why, yes! She plans an entirely new and larger kitchen." She leaned over to speak in conspiratorial tones. "Mr. Carlo has been ever so helpful in 'persuading' the city to speed up the process."

Mr. Jackson chuckled. "Why am I not surprised?" He ran a hand over Bessie's hair. "Then we shall visit."

He smiled to himself. "Hopefully without seeing Mr. Carlo."

This amused Mrs. Jackson no end. "And here I thought you loved everyone."

Mr. Jackson rolled his eyes, then picked up a book from the stack on the table. "Hardly."

"I suppose I don't blame you." She picked up a book from the table which looked interesting then turned to Duchess Cordelia. "Will you be coming with us?"

"Only if it's no bother."

Mr. Jackson looked up from his book. "Not at all! We insist." He closed the book, then put it on one side and moved Bessie to the other, leaning forward. "I promised dear old Albert I'd look after you, and you must be properly fed."

This seemed to delight the old woman. "Then I shall be honored."

Mrs. Jackson relaxed into her chair with a sigh. It felt good to be back, here in the hotel library she'd come to love so well.

The three read together in silence for some time. Then the clock struck half past eleven.

Mr. Jackson closed his book. "I think it best to go early, before the rush. Meet in the lobby at noon?"

Duchess Cordelia nodded. "I'll ring for Effie to help me get changed."

Mrs. Jackson checked out her books and the couple returned to their suite so she might put on her shawl. It was becoming chilly out. "We'll need winter jackets if we're to stay here for very long."

4

Mrs. Jackson followed Mr. Jackson and the dowager Duchess to a bistro with a gleaming glass storefront edged in brass.

Inside, small round tables and wooden chairs with delicate curved backs were set around the room, which was half-full. To the right, a long glass counter displayed a tempting delicatessen: meats, pastries, breads, fruit, and various cooked dishes. A sign on the counter read:

Buy Here, Eat There!

Quick, Easy Take-Out

Mrs. Jackson felt amazed. "What a novel concept!"

A woman with brown hair who appeared to be in her forties stood behind this counter. When she glanced over, she smiled, passing through a swinging door which came to her hips, and approached them, arms wide. "Goodness gracious! You should have told me you were in town."

Mrs. Jackson hugged her, then drew back to survey her. "Miss Goldie Jean. How splendid you look! And your shop!"

Her cheeks colored and she gave a shy smile. "I'm so glad you like it." She quickly recovered, though. "Come, sit wherever you like. Menus are on the tables. Just let me know when you're ready to order."

The room was brightly lit and cheerful. The couple chose a table across from the counter, along the wall.

Once they'd gotten their meals, Mrs. Jackson turned to Duchess Cordelia. "Now you must tell us everything which has gone on."

"I'm afraid my life has been uneventful. It's awfully lonesome these days with Albert gone. I like to visit the garden: it makes me feel closer to him."

Mrs. Jackson nodded.

"But something's happened at the Hotel. I'm certain of it."

Mr. Jackson said, "Going on?"

"Yes! Whispers and looking about this entire past week." Duchess Cordelia glanced around then leaned forward. "I'm hoping someone will spill the beans at dominoes tonight."

"It sounds most intriguing." Mr. Jackson took a sip of his coffee. "Hopefully it'll be something pleasant."

After lunch, the couple returned the Duchess to the Hotel, then went shopping for winter clothing. Mrs. Jackson especially loved the soft warm coats.

She found a cute little tan beaded handbag which matched the dresses she'd bought so far. She particularly liked its zippered pouch inside. So useful!

Around tea-time, they (and Bessie, and all their packages) went to a little stand and got something she'd never had before: the "hot dog". At first she felt dubious about the name. "What kind of meat is that?"

From the amused look on Mr. Jackson's face, he knew what she'd been thinking.

"These are entirely beef. You want pork, they got 'em around the corner." The man didn't seem to approve of his competitor's product. He turned to the next fellow. "You ready?"

She watched him put the meat in a bun and pile on vegetables and sauce. They smelled good. She turned to Mr. Jackson. "Let's split one."

So they did. "This is delicious," she said. "Why did they never sell these back home?"

Mr. Jackson just smiled at her.

Once, she'd thought her city was the center of the world. But now, seeing the sights, tasting all the delicious foods, doing things no one would ever have thought of there ... it made her almost glad she could never go back.

"What are you thinking about?"

She took his hand. "I love being here with you."

His cheeks colored, a shy smile upon his face. Yet his eyes grew moist. "That's the most wonderful thing anyone's ever told me."

She squeezed his hand. "Well, it's true." She slipped the little pinched end of her meat to Bessie, who set to it with vigor. "You've been here before in winter. What do you think we still need to buy?"

When the taxi pulled up to the Hotel, Harry was there to meet them. "I'll have Melvin bring these packages to your rooms."

"That's very kind of you," Mrs. Jackson said.

As Melvin and Harry piled the packages onto Melvin's cart, Mr. Jackson turned to her. "Want a soda?"

She did feel thirsty. "Yes, let's get one! I want to try strawberry this time."

Bessie kept pulling towards the other end of the circle drive. So Mrs. Jackson picked her up. "Come on,

Bessie," she said, and they went inside, to the soda shop on the right end of the lobby.

The last time they'd visited the Hotel, her Mr. Jackson had discovered the secret of the stuffed owl in the soda shop's far ceiling corner: when it blinked, this meant that a shipment of liquor had been delivered!

Neither of them had yet seen the speakeasy which must be somewhere below, but Mrs. Jackson felt sure it would be just as grand as what they'd seen so far.

As they sat at one of the cute little round tables sipping their sodas. Mrs. Jackson said, "May I ask something?"

Mr. Jackson set down his drink. "By all means."

"How did you know to meet me at the station?"

He chuckled. "The night we left home? My brother-in-law found out all about it and sent me word."

Mrs. Jackson glanced up to see him watching her, and his manner felt different than it had. It seemed as if he waited for her to explain what happened, why she went there. She sighed, feeling glum.

"You don't have to tell me if you don't want to," he said. "Just know that if you do want to, I'm here." His hand felt warm upon hers. "I care for you very much."

She nodded, yet felt a certain fear. She picked up Bessie from the floor and gave her a hug, eyes stinging.

She felt his hand warm upon hers. When she opened her eyes, he stood beside her. "It's almost time. You still want to see your friend?"

Mrs. Jackson smiled to herself. "I would." She set Bessie down, who had begun to struggle free. "Let's see how he's fared."

She felt excited at the prospect of seeing the new Chef, as well as a bit daunted. Would he remember her? And if he did, would he be glad to see her, or dismayed?

She and Mr. Jackson waited to one side of the staff's dining room as maids placed bowls of cut flowers upon the long trestle tables. Then the great Chef appeared.

He'd matured since last she saw him. He strode in, tall, confident, wearing a sky blue and white plaid shirt and black trousers. "You wished to see me?" Then realization dawned. "Mrs. —"

Mrs. Jackson quickly held up her hand. "Monsieur, please — here, we're called Mr and Mrs. Jackson."

The young man stared at the two, mouth open. "Is what they're saying true? Did you kill him?"

The horrible night not so long past came crashing in. *People think **I** killed him?* "No," she finally said. "But I was there. I — I was with him." What could she possibly give this man? "He didn't die alone."

The young Chef nodded, face downcast. "Thank you for telling me." Then he grasped her upper right arm, his eyes kind. "I'm so sorry for your loss."

For all the time that had passed, all the tears she'd cried, Mrs. Jackson still felt numb, as if perhaps it had been all a bad dream. "Thank you."

"Let's sit," the young Chef said, so they did. He clasped his hands on the table in front of him. "I've wanted to thank you for the opportunity to come here."

Mrs. Jackson glanced at Mr. Jackson, who smiled softly. "When my wife told me about you, it seemed the perfect solution to the Hotel's difficulty."

Mrs. Jackson leaned forward, and in an instant she knew what she needed. "Are you happy?"

The young Monsieur seemed to consider this most seriously. "I am."

He leaned back, and in his voice lay a hint of his time in Paris. "The first few days were difficult, me being young enough to be their child. Grand-child, for some. And for all my years of experience, this was my first time to be in actual charge of the kitchens. A few thought it wrong to let the former Cook go, and they put their anger upon me."

He glanced aside, a small smile upon his face. "But I gathered my entire staff together the day I took charge and said, 'I was brought here to prosper you. If you can't take my commands, speak before we close today, and I'll release you with a good recommendation. Defy me henceforth, and matters won't go so well.'"

Mrs. Jackson gasped. "How did you dare speak so?"

The young Chef smiled to himself. "I merely considered what the men I'd trained under since I was a boy would have said, then softened it by half." He chuckled at that. "My masters have been fierce, formidable men. But wise, for the most part." He glanced away. "And we've prospered, for which I'm grateful."

"As are we," Mr. Jackson said. "I know we've never met before, Monsieur, but my wife has spoken of you enough that I feel I know you."

This seemed to amuse the young Chef no end. "I hope your opinion of me is mostly good."

"It is," Mr. Jackson said.

Good smells came from the kitchen, and men began setting the tables, George among them.

Mrs. Jackson rose, and the men did as well. "We should let you get your dinner." On impulse, she hugged the Chef, recalling the first time she'd met him, long ago. "I'm very, very proud of you."

He smiled shyly, eyes reddening. "I wouldn't be here except for you. For that, I'm forever grateful."

5

M r. Raymond arrived right on time to dress Mr. Jackson for dinner. He laid out his shaving kit, selected Mr. Jackson's dinner suit, and prepared a hot towel just as usual. But after Mr. Jackson seated himself for the shave, Mr. Raymond frowned.

"What is it?"

"Your neck." He fished out a small mirror. "A blemish has formed there."

Mr. Jackson felt amused. "I haven't had one of those since I was a boy."

"You're very fortunate." He applied the hot towel, then turned to his kit, took out some instruments, and small jars of various colors. "It's happens a lot, especially in men with such coiled hair as yours."

Mr. Jackson relaxed into the chair as Mr. Raymond lathered his face, sharpened his straight razor, and began his work.

Mr. Raymond finally said, "There! Good as new."

Mr. Jackson took up the mirror. The blemished area was reduced in size and had been covered by a paste closely matching his dark skin. "Must I do anything?"

"Wash your neck with soap and apply another hot towel before bed. That and a good night's sleep should take care of it. But I'll check on it in the morning."

The couple, having been suitably attired, went down to dinner. To Mrs. Jackson's surprise and delight, the Chef sent out a special plate with her favorite foods: roasted ham glazed with honey and cloves, potatoes mashed with garlic and butter, sweet pickles, and a fine crystal cup holding lime sorbet.

After dinner, the couple joined Duchess Cordelia in her suite for dominoes.

Many of the maids, waiters, and other staff were there, most already seated around the spacious parlor. Their waiter for breakfast, Will, was there. And George Neuberg, of course, as well as their bell boy Melvin and the red-haired valet they'd seen parking cars the other night, whose name turned out to be Harry.

Other friends were there as well. Helen ran a nearby pastry shop, and was newly married to Mr. Jackson's friend Eugene, who did the "dirty work" around the Hotel. Duchess Cordelia introduced Effie, the maid for their floor, who doubled as her lady's maid.

Mr. Jackson introduced a young man named Stanley — who happened to be Effie's older brother — as his new manservant. Bessie immediately went to Stanley and put her little paws up on his shin, tail wagging.

He gave Bessie a fond smile and petted her head.

"You're the fellow who lost the gem in your tie-clasp," Mrs. Jackson said. "A pleasure to meet you."

"Yes, ma'am," Stanley said.

"Well, we've looked all round," Mrs. Jackson said.

"As did I," said Effie.

"I'm sure it'll turn up," Mr. Jackson said.

But not everyone was there. Mr. Lee Francis was home with his wife and new son. The young Head Chef had begged off, saying he did little after close and cleanup but to fall into his bed. "The work is entirely taxing. But I feel stronger with each day. Perhaps in the future, I'll join you."

"It seems everyone knows everyone," Mrs. Jackson said, a bit daunted by the thought. Somehow, her Mr. Jackson seemed to know them all already. How did he do it?

Effie smiled at her, holding out a hand. "Well, now you know us all too. Come, sit here by us."

So she did! Mrs. Jackson had never played dominoes before, but the rules weren't difficult to learn and she was soon winning from time to time. She noticed her Mr. Jackson and George whispering together through most of the game, and she suspected he didn't know how to play any more than she had.

Bessie had the run of the suite until she put her paws up on Melvin, who shied away from her. "I don't like dogs much."

"Forgive me," Mrs. Jackson said. "Bessie! Over here." She picked up the little dog and clipped on the leash, keeping her close by.

The party seemed quite the success. Those there were full of gossip about the doings in the Hotel, which Mrs. Jackson found mostly amusing.

When someone mentioned the Hotel manager, though, the dowager Duchess frowned, crossing her arms in front of her. "I'd prefer not to speak of that man, if you please."

The others glanced at each other and fell silent. It seemed clear that Duchess Cordelia Stayman still blamed Mr. Flannery Davis for the unfortunate events which took place during the last time the couple had stayed at the Hotel.

But soon everyone was talking and laughing again. And the biggest topic of discussion was the Head Valet: the man, it seemed, had gone missing.

6

Mrs. Jackson said, "I've seen him, but I don't believe we've ever been introduced."

Mr. Raymond said, "His name's Earl Vincenzo. Odious fellow."

"He is not," Effie said in a teasing tone. "Lately, he's been rather sweet. Besides, I thought you were friends."

Mr. Raymond rolled his eyes and crossed his arms.

George said, "Vincenzo's still not back?"

Many shook their heads.

Eugene leaned forward. "And no one will say anything about it."

"One minute he was there," Harry said, "the next, he was gone." He seemed daunted by this.

Mrs. Jackson said, "And no one's seen him since?" It seemed a mystery, to be sure.

"Good riddance." Maria had been promoted to Head Maid since last the couple had visited. "Always come in barking at people like he owned the place. And always bothering my maids." She gave Effie a quick glance. "Probably run off with some girl or other."

Effie looked uncomfortable.

Melvin pushed up his round spectacles. "Wonder who'll replace him."

"They better do it soon," Harry said. "It's been a week now, and all confusion since."

How strange, Mrs. Jackson thought. "Does he often go missing?"

They all looked at each other.

Eugene said, "No, come to think of it. He never has."

***

Mr. Jackson watched his wife as she played. The change that had come over her since they left for their trip amazed him. She smiled now. She even seemed to be making friends here.

He recalled how her face crumpled at the young Chef's mere mention of the night her first husband died.

She's still not recovered, he thought.

Nor should she be, he decided, recalling his own terrible loss long before.

Travel seemed good for her. He'd not wanted to leave. But might more travel help her?

After several rounds of dominoes, a knock came at the parlor door. Room service had arrived, with various sorts of food and drink. Duchess Cordelia announced a refreshment break, instructing the waiters to place the assortment upon the table and dresser in the bedroom.

Mr. Jackson stood, stretching. The games were lively and the conversation good, but he needed to move about. He found George by the drink table, setting out the cups. "There you are!"

George turned to him with a smile. "That last play was a good one!" His face turned mischievous and sly. "But I'll win next time!"

Mr. Jackson laughed. "I take up the challenge, sir!" Then he sobered. "Let me ask you something: how about you come with us on our next trip?"

George's manner cooled; he glanced away, giving a half-hearted shrug. "I don't know ..."

"Can't you get off work?"

George's shoulders twitched. He stuck his hands in his pockets, eyes upon the floor. "Sure, I could, but ..."

Mr. Jackson wasn't sure what was wrong. "You don't have to answer now. I'm not even sure where we'll be off to next." He smiled to himself. "We'll probably be here for a while. Just wanted to make the offer."

George nodded, eyes still upon the floor. "Thanks." He clapped Mr. Jackson on the arm, not looking at him. "Be right back." He went towards the bathroom.

Mr. Jackson loitered there at the table for several minutes. When George didn't return, Mr. Jackson knocked on the door. "You all right in there?"

"Go on, you goof," George said lightly. "I'm fine."

Smiling to himself, Mr. Jackson went to check on his wife.

Mrs. Jackson stood out on the parlor balcony smoking, gazing out over the lake-shore. Bessie lay curled up at her feet. She turned at his approach. "Enjoying yourself?"

He put an arm over her shoulder. "I am." Then he recalled he'd never asked her. "You mind if we bring George with us the next time we travel?"

His wife chuckled. "I thought you wanted never to ever leave."

He turned to face her, leaning on the wrought iron railing. "Well ... it depends."

She gave him a wry, knowing smile. "I see!" She let out a short laugh. "Sure! Bring him along! I like George."

"Do you?"

"Very much." She took a drag on her cigarette, blew out smoke, staring out over the shoreline. "He reminds me a bit of myself at that age." She turned to face him, leaning upon the rail. "Hopefully, he'll turn out better than I did."

Mr. Jackson studied the lovely curves of her face, lit by both the room behind and the buildings before her. He tucked a curl around her ear. "I don't think you turned out so badly."

He loved watching her blush, the barely shy smile.

Cordelia called out, "Want to play more?"

They went inside. Mr. Jackson looked around. "Where's George?"

Cordelia said, "Wasn't feeling well, the poor dear. He went home."

Mr. Jackson said, "I'm sorry to hear that."

He seemed okay a few minutes back, Mr. Jackson thought. If he's not here tomorrow, I'll look in on him.

"It's your play, sir," Cordelia said, and all thoughts on the matter were forgotten.

***

When the couple returned to their suite, they sat for a time in the parlor, Bessie curled up on the floor between them. Mrs. Jackson said, "What do you think about this missing Head Valet?"

Mr. Jackson shrugged. "It's really none of our concern. My only hope is that the Hotel will choose someone a bit more agreeable next time."

"You don't like him?"

He seemed to seriously consider this. "I've only come across him twice now, yet each time I felt uneasy." He shook his head, gave a one-shoulder shrug. "He's done nothing to offend. It's just ..."

Mrs. Jackson nodded, not understanding but trying to. Mr. Jackson's mind often seemed to run in different circles than hers. "How's your new manservant?"

"Perfectly well. I prefer Mr. Vienna, but this man is capable enough."

Something about the way he'd said it ... "Yet he also makes you uneasy."

Mr. Jackson straightened, took a deep breath and let it out. "Well, to be honest, yes." He shrugged, then smiled down at their little dog, who'd put her paws upon his leg. "Bessie seems to like him, at any rate."

He reached down to smooth her hair, then set the little dog beside him. "It's nothing I can pin on the man, but I'll be very glad when Mr. Vienna returns. Perhaps it's just that I'm more used to him."

"When Mr. Vienna does return, you should request him on a more permanent basis."

Mr. Jackson's face brightened. "An excellent idea! Yes, that would be splendid. I'll speak with Mr. Vienna about it the moment he arrives."

***

The next morning, Mr. Jackson felt more rested, and in a much better humor. But instead of getting better, his neck now had several blemishes upon it.

Mr. Raymond shook his head. "I can try an oil treatment. But in cases like this the best course is to let the hair grow. Have you ever fancied a beard?"

Mr. Jackson shrugged. "Never considered it. But if you think it'll help ..."

"I do."

"Then just trim round the edges as you can."

When the couple went down to breakfast, the tables in the back third of the room had been changed. Instead of the usual large round tables, there now sat dozens of square tables which seated four. The dining room was packed: they got the last two seats in a round table of sallow-faced men who chattered to each other in a language he didn't understand.

George was there that morning, stationed far across the room. Yet he looked haggard, and too focused upon his work, as if he'd not slept.

"I hope he's well," Mr. Jackson said.

"We all have our down times," his wife said. "He'll be his old self again."

Mr. Jackson thought about that. "Duchess Cordelia said he went home ill. You don't think so?"

His wife shrugged. "You know him better than I."

He considered this the entire meal, running back over the conversation he'd had with George in his mind. He couldn't think of what he might have said which would trouble George so.

Perhaps he was feeling ill even then, and didn't wish to speak of it.

Mr. Jackson sipped his coffee, which tasted especially good this morning. *You're fussing like an old woman*. His wife had been entirely correct: whatever was the matter, George would soon be well.

He chuckled at himself. In any case, if he'd said something to offend, George would surely say so.

His wife said, "What amuses you?"

"Oh, it seems people act in their own certain way. We're all quite predictable."

She gave an ironic little snort of amusement. "Until we're not."

"Oh?"

"That Head Valet, for example. Everyone's saying he'd never run off, yet there he's gone." She raised her hand for the waiter. "Might I get more tea?"

Mr. Jackson mused upon what his wife had said, then he took up her hand and kissed it. "These puzzles do occupy your mind." Was she so focused on this Head Valet simply to forget her own sorrows?

She smiled warmly at him. "Are you feeling neglected, sir?"

The group of travelers rose, so he did as well. They left without so much as acknowledging him, which seemed rather rude. He sat, finishing his coffee as he pondered his wife's question. "Not that I can detect."

She leaned towards him. "Let's spend the day together, as we did before we left here last."

"That sounds like an excellent idea."

After breakfast, the couple decided to go for a stroll in the park near to the Hotel. Bessie was quite enthusiastic about this idea.

Mr. Jackson said, "Did you enjoy the time last night, dear?"

His wife blew out smoke and tapped the ashes from her cigarette. "I did. I'm looking forward to playing again next week."

Bessie's curly black hair had been last cut several weeks back. "When we get back, let's see if the groomer has room for our girl today."

His wife looked down and laughed. "She is looking a bit mop-like, isn't she?"

The day was bright and cool, the sun having a touch of orange to it even at this early hour. He'd only been here once in winter, and that only for a day.

Perhaps they'd go south this trip, he thought. That is, when George was feeling well again. The Caribbean was said to be lovely this time of year. They'd have to go before the weather turned bad ...

"Did you want to go there now?"

With a start, Mr. Jackson realized they'd come round the park. It was either around once more, or back to the hotel. He checked his watch: half past eleven. "Let's see if they can fit her in."

They walked back to the Hotel and across the wide lobby to the right, where a hallway led past the elevators. A hall on the right read:

Dog Grooming & Veterinary Services

The veterinarian stood at the counter rifling through papers. He glanced up when they entered. "Good morning! I hope all's well?"

"Certainly," Mrs. Jackson said. "Might we get Bessie a trim?"

The man beamed. "Right this way!"

The veterinarian's wife was the groomer. When they entered her back room, she was leading a Great Dane to his owner. That done, she smiled at them then said to Bessie, "Time for your bath?"

Mr. Jackson handed over the leash. "As the youngsters say, she needs a hairdo."

The woman said, "I'll take care of everything."

He said, "When shall we return?"

"Oh, a bath and a clip won't be more than an hour. But take all the time you need. My boys'll look after her."

The couple went back to the lobby, intending to look around the gift shop, which they'd not yet had a chance to visit. But the owner of the Hotel spied them, striding purposefully in their direction.

"I wonder what he wants," Mr. Jackson said, feeling disgruntled.

"Now, now," his wife said. "No need to keep grudges."

He thought that possibly right. Yet the man was insufferable!

Mr. Montgomery Carlo was a swarthy heavyset man with hooded brown eyes, who held a black walking-stick tipped in brass. "So good to see you again!" He held out his hand. "Might I have a word with you — just for a moment?"

Mr. Jackson shook the man's hand, if a bit grudgingly. "Very well."

The couple followed Mr. Carlo out to the front. This time of day, traffic in the street was brisk and noisy. Yet in the circle drive there was little activity.

Two valets he hadn't met yet, one black-haired, the other blond, stood talking. Harry leaned on the Head Valet's podium ten feet away, nodding to them when they glanced over.

Mr. Jackson said to Mr. Carlo, "How may we help?"

"I'm sure you've heard by now about my missing Head Valet."

"We have," Mr. Jackson said.

Mr. Carlo shook his head. "The police have absolutely no interest in the matter. And he's been gone over a week!"

Mrs. Jackson sounded impressed. "It's very kind of you to have such concern for your employees."

"It's more than that. Earl's my first cousin —"

Mrs. Jackson said, "Oh?"

" — and he wouldn't run off. Not in the middle of a shift, and certainly not without telling someone where he'd gone."

Two cars drove up past them and parked just past the Head Valet's podium. Harry pressed a button there.

Mrs. Jackson nodded. "I understand, sir. And I sympathize! But it's not unusual for Missing Persons cases to be of low priority. In adults, that is."

Mr. Jackson felt a flash of pride in her knowledge of such matters.

Mr. Carlo drew back, chagrined. "So what can I do?" Then his face turned determined. "You must help me."

Melvin came outside, hurrying up to the first car. A second bellhop followed.

Mr. Jackson spoke quietly. "The last time we helped you, Mr. Carlo, you tried to blackmail us. Why should we help you now?"

Mrs. Jackson stared at him as if he'd gone mad.

But it was true!

Mr. Carlo said, "Sir, I — I humbly apologize for my behavior. Please forgive me."

The man must really be worried. "Oh, very well."

Mr. Carlo looked relieved.

"But only if we're kept entirely out of any publicity."

"You have my word," said Mr. Carlo.

Mrs. Jackson said, "Where was he last seen?"

Mr. Carlo gestured to the other end of the circle drive some thirty feet off, where cars would leave to merge onto the city street. A third car had pulled up behind the first two. "He went into the alleyway there and hasn't been seen since."

Mrs. Jackson said, "Then we must see this alleyway!"

His wife was all too eager to solve a puzzle. At times, it amused him. Today, he felt annoyed.

I'm still angry at Mr. Carlo, he thought.

He took a deep breath, let it out. The man's family had disappeared. He should at least look.

Harry came jogging into view. A large group streamed out of the Hotel, turning towards them.

So Mr. Jackson followed Mr. Carlo past the cars, the young valets, the crowd of people, the bellboys and their loads of luggage, to stand on the sidewalk in front of a long, graveled alleyway.

The alley went straight through to the far street past two stretches of wall. The wall on the left was three stories of brick, the hotel's wall on the right was stone, thirty-three stories high. The alley ran for a good city block, with not so much as a window on either side until he looked up. Six stories above them, the Hotel's balconies began.

Mr. Jackson felt astonished. Where could the man have gone? "Are you certain he went this way?"

"Three of my valets saw him turn the corner," Mr. Carlo said. Then he looked up at each side. "I've even had men go to the roof and balconies to look for rope." He shook his head. "Nothing." Mr. Carlo poked his walking-stick into the gravel. "Only goes down a few inches — hardly enough to hide a body."

"Oh, dear," Mrs. Jackson said. "Don't think that, not yet."

Mr. Jackson took his wife's arm. "Very well. Let's see this alleyway. Perhaps there's something about it we're missing."

***

Mrs. Jackson clung to Mr. Jackson's arm as they crunched over the gravel. Where could the man have possibly gone to?

The alley ran without break: walls, gravel, sky.

It was as if the man had disappeared.

She'd seen gravel many a time. Yet she'd never walked on the stuff before, and she hated the way it gave way beneath her feet. It shifted, made unpleasant sounds as she moved. "Surely someone heard him walk on this."

Mr. Jackson said, "At mid-day, with traffic like it is? Hardly. Listen."

They stopped, and from here — perhaps twenty yards down — they could barely hear the traffic.

A chill came over her. A man could have shouted, screamed, and not been heard.

The three crunched along to the end of the long alley. No grates lay on either side.

Did this alley have no drainage?

She decided a grate would have let the gravel just drop through. The path ran smooth and complete.

Perhaps they put down gravel to cover up flooding, she thought, so it wouldn't be muddy.

Along the left was brick all the way to the wide, tree-lined street. But the fine stone of the Hotel ended some thirty yards to the right along the drop down to the dock, with a metal railing painted black spanning the distance. Far below, men and trucks and loads moved in a flurry of activity.

They crunched over to the sidewalk and turning round it, surveyed the dock. From this vantage, there were three levels. A platform at street level had stairs descending fifteen feet on either side to the parking lot.

To the left, several trucks were parked at a loading dock. A truck pulled up a driveway on the far side of the lot and turned to drive away.

To the right, another truck backed down an underground driveway to a second loading dock large enough to fit three trucks there.

"He was supposed to meet some of my dockworkers there." Mr. Carlo pointed across to the platform. "They were to have lunch together —"

Mrs. Jackson noticed several electric lamps above the platform. Of course, they were turned off at this time of day, but what surprised her was that one of the glass covers was blue!

"— but he never arrived. Twenty minutes they waited. But when they walked through to the front to find him, he was gone."

It didn't take twenty minutes to walk back here. Surely someone would have seen Mr. Vincenzo if he'd emerged. Mrs. Jackson gazed down the alleyway. "I have no answer for you, sir."

This seemed a puzzle greater than any she'd solved yet. "Men don't just disappear. There must be something else going on."

"I'll walk back with you," Mr. Carlo said. "Through the alley, or brave the docks?"

The docks seemed all a-flurry. Another truck passed them to turn into the driveway. Men were carrying boxes up the steps to the platform on both sides.

"Perhaps the alley," Mr. Jackson said.

A car came slowly crunching up the alley, and as it approached, they stepped aside to let it pass. Mrs. Jackson said, "Does this way have much traffic?"

"No," Mr. Carlo said. "It's too sharp a corner to turn the trucks into the dock, so most go the long way round. Just the occasional car."

A family sat in the car: three children and a couple. The husband hunched over the steering wheel, peering this way and that before turning left.

Mr. Carlo chuckled. "It's likely that he's lost."

As they retraced their steps, Mrs. Jackson remembered the brochure she'd seen when they arrived to the Hotel. "Didn't this alley used to have cobblestones?"

Mr. Carlo shrugged. "I suppose the City Planning Office might know."

Mrs. Jackson felt her foot suddenly slip into the gravel, and something grated along the heel of her right shoe. She stopped, lifted her foot. A deep gouge over a half-inch long rose up along the leather covering her heel. "My shoes are ruined by this stuff!"

Mr. Jackson said, "We'll get you another pair."

"I suppose." She trudged along, feeling disgruntled. She liked those shoes. "But why would Mr. Vincenzo come down this alley at mid-day wearing his good shoes when he could have just gone through the Hotel?"

Mr. Carlo stopped, astonishment on his face. "You're right!"

"You know, I'd never considered that," Mr. Jackson said, at almost the same time.

They stared at each other.

Mrs. Jackson struggled along through the gravel, clinging to Mr. Jackson's arm. "There must have been some reason for it." She peered up at the blank walls beside them, feeling as though she missed something.

When they arrived back at the front of the Hotel, Mrs. Jackson said, "Might I speak to the valets here? With your permission, Mr. Carlo, of course."

Mr. Carlo said, "Whatever you need." Then he disappeared into the Hotel.

"Let's get you into some other shoes," Mr. Jackson said, "then we can pick up Bessie."

While she put on a new pair, Mr. Jackson leaned against her dresser, her damaged shoes in hand. "If you really like these shoes, I can have them repaired. Whatever makes you happy."

He was a dear man. "Only if it's no trouble."

"None at all! I'll call right down. They can send the maid for our floor to have it taken care of."

Mrs. Jackson smiled at him. "I appreciate it."

When the couple came out of the elevators, they went left, then turned down the narrower hall to their right to retrieve Bessie from the groomer.

Mrs. Jackson felt a great fondness for her little dog. "Why, you've had a haircut! Don't you look pretty?"

Bessie danced with excitement.

Returning to the larger hallway, the three turned left past the elevators. They then went to the lobby and the gift shop which lay in its left corner, close to the street.

The gift shop had all sorts of items one might expect: souvenirs of the Hotel, as well as of the city. Toiletries and patent medicines, fresh flowers, small gifts. After so much travel, to her it seemed ordinary. But Mr. Jackson appeared enthralled, examining each item in turn.

Mrs. Jackson handed Bessie's leash to him. "You stay as long as you like. I think I'll talk with the valets."

Mr. Jackson gave her a happy smile, then went back to examining a golden wristwatch.

So Mrs. Jackson returned to the front of the hotel. Traffic had slowed in the time they'd been gone. Harry waited alone at the valet box, so she approached him. "Sir, might I have a word? Mr. Carlo has approved it."

"Of course."

"You said last night that Mr. Vincenzo was there last week," she pointed the way she'd just come, "and then he was gone."

"Yes, ma'am. I saw him standing there. Well, it was back closer to the wall. Then a car came up, and I took the man's keys. When I looked back, Mr. Earl was gone."

"What happened then? Anything unusual?"

The young man stood in thought for a moment. "When I pulled out to park the car, a truck turned in front of me into the alley. It was all very sudden: he didn't signal or nothing. I had to slam on my brakes."

"One of yours?"

"Yeah," he said, as if he hadn't realized it before. "It was strange. No one drives trucks down there. Even with the small ones you have to do a three-point turn to get into the dock."

Mrs. Jackson had never driven a car, but she understood what he meant. Something definitely wasn't right. "Did you happen to look down the alley?"

"No, ma'am, I didn't. It was busy out. You have to keep your wits about you to get parking here!"

Right then, Mr. Carlo, Mr. Jackson, and Bessie came out through the front doors to the Hotel. Bessie seemed very happy to see her!

A car pulled up. Harry said, "I best get back to work."

"Thanks for your help."

The three approached her. Mr. Carlo said, "Did you learn anything?"

"Well, yes," Mrs. Jackson said. "A truck went down the alley a short time after Mr. Vincenzo did."

Mr. Jackson put his hand to his chin, "So they could have picked up Mr. Vincenzo or seen what happened."

Mrs. Jackson gestured to Harry, who stood with an older gentleman beside a gleaming new car. "He said the truck was one of yours. He should be able to tell you which one."

Harry got into the car and drove off.

"I'll speak with him when he returns," Mr. Carlo said. "Each truck is assigned to a crew. They should be able to tell me what they saw, if anything."

Mrs. Jackson said to Mr. Jackson, "Did you end up getting anything?"

He gave Mr. Carlo a quick glance. "A gift for a friend. I had it sent up to the room."

Bessie began sniffing their shoes, then pulled towards the graveled alley, whining.

"You know, she's done that twice since we arrived," Mrs. Jackson said. "I wonder what she smells."

The three of them followed Bessie to the gravel, then down the alleyway. About ten yards along, Bessie moved to the center of the alleyway and began growling.

When Bessie began to dig, Mrs. Jackson snatched the little dog away from the sharp gravel. "No, Bessie, dear, you'll hurt yourself!"

Mr. Jackson stood staring at the place Bessie had been digging, horror on his face. "We need a shovel." He turned, running towards the street.

Mrs. Jackson took a step back. "Mr. Carlo, perhaps you should join him." She looked over at the man, who'd gone pale. "If your cousin is in there, you don't want to see him."

Bessie strained in her arms, growling, barking.

"Hush," Mrs. Jackson said, petting her little dog. "You've done your duty, and that very well."

The black and brass walking-stick clattered to the ground. Mr. Carlo retreated to the wall, hands clasped to his face.

Soon men came with shovels, and under the gravel there was a manhole, propped open with a bit of gravel. They then called for crowbars, and after some effort, removed the cover.

Underneath, it was as they'd feared.

Mr. Earl Vincenzo lay below, gravel all around him, dead.

7

Mrs. Jackson held Bessie as she, Mr. Jackson, and Mr. Carlo stood on the sidewalk watching the crime scene.

Mr. Carlo had his fists firmly planted on his hips. "So **now** the police are interested," he said bitterly. "If they'd done their job, my cousin might've been found the day he disappeared. Perhaps even alive!"

The alleyway had been cordoned off at the street on both ends, with officers directing curious passerby around the area. Inside the cordon, a truck marked "Coroner" sat parked facing the street. In the alley beyond, a flurry of activity.

Sergeant Benjamin Nestor approached the couple, shaking his head. "You again."

Mr. Carlo pressed forward. "What happened?"

"Hit on the head, looks like," the sergeant said. "But it's a good ten feet down there. Still don't know if it was the blow to the head or the fall that killed him. The coroner will have his report to us in a few days."

"I'm calling his wife," Mr. Carlo said.

The sergeant watched him leave. "All this time I thought he'd run off."

"You're a homicide man," Mr. Jackson said. "How'd you know about this?"

"Carlo had me on the phone not thirty seconds after my patrolman left, wanting to make sure he got proper service." The sergeant let out a short laugh, then sobered. "I suppose he's got you two investigating now."

"Only just," said Mr. Jackson. "But my wife did learn something useful."

Mrs. Jackson felt amused at the dubious expression on the sergeant's face. "I spoke with one of the valets. A Hotel truck went down the alley minutes after the man did. It's a full block to the other side: surely whoever drove that truck saw him."

The sergeant nodded. "I'll have my men talk with them. I've also sent men to see where those tunnels go. If he climbed down and someone killed him, there'll be some sign of them along the way."

Mrs. Jackson shook her head. "Someone replaced the manhole, filled in around it, and smoothed it out. That took time. Whoever was on that truck either saw Mr. Vincenzo and the man who killed him, or did the deed themselves."

Mr. Jackson had been frowning, hand to chin. "The hole isn't that very far from the street. Surely someone saw something."

To Mrs. Jackson's dismay, the sergeant laughed. "Here? Even if someone were to watch the entire deed, they'd not tell me. No, sir, while we police do our best, the Mob has too much influence here." He shrugged. "For all we know, they could have done this themselves."

Mr. Jackson said, "Mr. Carlo has asked us to help. But what would you have us do?"

"As little as you must," the sergeant said. "But if you do learn something, bring it to me first. Carlo's too invested in this matter to be rational."

Mrs. Jackson nodded. In his state, Mr. Carlo might shoot someone they merely considered a suspect.

Then the sergeant twitched. "There is one thing. The wife. I'm sure she knows something, but she won't talk to me."

Mrs. Jackson felt surprised. "You want **me** to?"

"If you would. Perhaps she'd talk to you."

Mrs. Jackson took a step back, heart pounding. Talk to a grieving widow about her murdered husband? Her voice shook. "I don't know if I can."

Sergeant Nestor frowned. "You're ever the sticky-beak when it's not wanted. Now I actually need your help and you say no?"

Bessie struggled a bit in her arms, growling.

To her surprise, Mr. Jackson said, "I won't have my wife harassed! She's still in mourning!"

Sergeant Nestor's eyes narrowed, as if trying to recall something.

"You've asked," Mr. Jackson said sternly. "If and when she feels able, she'll do so." He put his arm around her shoulders. "Until then, good day to you."

"Well, then," the sergeant said, and it seemed clear he felt disgruntled. "I should return to work."

Mrs. Jackson set Bessie down, the leash looped around her wrist. Overwhelmed with grief and remorse, she buried her face in Mr. Jackson's chest.

His arms went warm around her. "I'm sorry he did that. It was thoughtless and unfair."

She turned her head to one side, another wave of grief washing over her before she could speak. "Thank you for defending me." It was so different from the man she once thought him to be. She put her arms round him, eyes shut, listening to the people passing by on all sides. Then she took a handkerchief from her pocket and wiped underneath her eyes.

He smiled fondly at her, then took her face in his hands and kissed her forehead. "We'll get through this." He glanced down. "Won't we, Bessie?"

Smiling to herself, Mrs. Jackson stuffed the handkerchief back into her pocket.

The couple turned arm in arm to face the lake, and slowly, her mind began to clear. Her gaze fell across the wide Lake Shore Drive and onto the lovely benches stationed there. She nudged Mr. Jackson, gesturing towards them. "Are you thinking what I'm thinking?"

"I believe I am."

For the next few days, the couple took Bessie down to the stoplight, across Lake Shore Drive, then back. They sat upon the benches at the time the murder must have occurred.

But while they saw many a person cross the graveled alley, only one crossed every day: a young woman wearing a cloche hat and coat the color of dark mustard.

The next day, Mrs. Jackson followed her.

8

The woman was short with strawberry blonde curls. She walked quickly, with purpose, never looking back, then darted between two buildings.

When Mrs. Jackson peered around the corner into the cobblestone alleyway, the woman stood right there, arms crossed.

Mrs. Jackson jumped back, startled. "Oh!"

She was young, perhaps twenty, with hazel eyes. "I thought you were checking on me," the woman said, "rather than just going my way. Who are you? And why are you following?"

"I mean you no harm." Mrs. Jackson stepped forward, out of view of the street. "But you go past the Hotel every day. In that alley where the police have been, did you see anything go on last week?"

A cynical look crossed the woman's face. "With the police, are you?"

"Not actually," Mrs. Jackson said. "The family asked me to help." For a moment, she'd forgotten what she was called here. But then she held out a hand. "Pamela Jackson."

The woman's eyebrows raised, but she briefly took Mrs. Jackson's hand, her unbuttoned coat falling open. "A lady investigator? You don't see that every day."

"Mostly retired." This girl wasn't one of the waifs displayed in the papers: a fine form lay under that cute little dress she wore. "But my Mr. Jackson and I are acquainted with the family, so —"

The woman let out a soft chuckle. "You've been pressed into service." She gave a quick flick of her chin. "The husband works with you, I take it?"

Mrs. Jackson shrugged. "We're just newly married."

The woman appraised her. "You seem a decent enough sort. Sure, I saw a truck there last week. I noticed it because there hasn't been one there for a long while."

"Now that **is** interesting. How long ago were other trucks there?"

The woman smiled. "Oh, back when there used to be cobbles in that alley. And that's all I'll say on that topic, thank you very much."

Hmm, Mrs. Jackson thought.

"Don't look for me later. I'll be taking a new route to work from now on."

Mrs. Jackson blurted out, "Then I shall be grieved. You're the most interesting person I've met here so far."

The woman's cheeks colored, and she gave a wry little smile. "Am I now?" For an instant, the woman surveyed her. "Perhaps I might not disappear entirely."

For the first time in a long while, Mrs. Jackson felt flustered. "Please don't. I beg you, pray join us for dinner. As amends for having caused you distress."

"Dinner? At that grand hotel?" The woman chuckled. "I'd have nothing to wear."

"Luncheon?"

The woman considered it. "Perhaps." Then she straightened, spoke with confidence. "I believe I will."

Mrs. Jackson felt relieved. "Tomorrow, then? Just give your name to the Headwaiter."

"It would be a pleasure."

"I'm truly sorry to have disturbed you."

The woman gave a soft smile. "The name's Ophelia. Denton. But if anyone else comes looking, I never saw you in my life."

***

While Mrs. Jackson was following Miss Ophelia Denton, Mr. Jackson decided to speak to the Hotel's manager.

Mr. Flannery Davis sat behind his desk, glancing up at Mr. Jackson's knock upon the open door. "Good day, sir. How may I help?"

Mr. Jackson tucked Bessie under his left arm. "Might we speak privately, sir?"

"Of course. Close the door, there, will you?"

Mr. Jackson closed the door and sat across the desk from the man, settling Bessie on his lap. "I know about your little speakeasy downstairs."

The man paled for a moment, but quickly recovered. "Are you going to tell the Feds?"

"Certainly not!" Mr. Jackson and his wife wanted nothing to do with the Feds. "Yet I also know that your former Head Valet had some dealings with those supplying you."

"Oh," the manager said, realization dawning in his face. "And you think he may have offended them?"

"Hard to say, not knowing what his involvement was. But Mr. Carlo's quite anxious to learn who's done this, so —"

"You're here on his behalf."

"I felt it better to speak with you about this, rather than him. The whole thing must be a terrible ordeal."

"Indeed." The manager nodded slowly, eyes on his desk. Then he raised his head. "When a shipment comes in, we have a signal —"

The blinking owl in the soda shop.

"— which Mr. Vincenzo can — um, could — see from his station. At that point, he collected the staff together to unload the trucks."

"So the entire staff is in on this?"

"Most believe it's a delivery like any other. Many of the youngsters know about the speakeasy, but —"

"Not that they're helping to supply it."

"No. Only our most trusted men know what's in the crates we receive."

"Let me get this straight. Mr. Vincenzo was simply in charge of collecting workers to unload trucks. Am I correct? Or did he have a bigger role?"

"Well ... he'd look out for the Feds, or anyone he suspected of being with them. There's a blue light out back. If that goes on —"

Mr. Jackson recalled the trucks backing down to the lower dock. "The trucks drive away."

"Exactly."

It sounded as if the only people who might take offense at what the man was doing were the Feds themselves. Hardly the sort of fellows who'd knock a man senseless then throw him into the sewers. "Well, thanks for speaking with me."

"My pleasure."

"And thank you for your kindness."

"Oh, that, sir. Never you mind. Mr. Carlo's family first came here as outsiders, and he saw how your people — and his — were treated first thing. We had a talk about it when I was hired. You have money, you are more than welcome here."

Mr. Jackson smiled, but he didn't feel it. He'd first come here after he had his men investigate the place, and while it was indeed as fine as it seemed, his first few visits — while comfortable indeed — had not been nearly so welcoming.

When he first brought his wife here, injured as she was, it was the best he might manage on such short notice. But her accompanying him seemed to have made all the difference. "Very good." He rose, setting Bessie onto the floor. "I'll let you get back to work."

***

Mrs. Jackson met back with Mr. Jackson for an early luncheon, which they took in the Hotel dining room. But before they might share all they'd learned, the dowager Duchess appeared!

"Oh, my dear friends! You should have told me you were coming early! I would have met you at once." She surveyed Mr. Jackson's face. "Oh, I do love the beard!"

Mrs. Jackson smiled to herself. "Won't you join us?"

"Only if it won't be an imposition," Duchess Cordelia said.

"We insist," Mr. Jackson said. "In fact, I would welcome your thoughts on a matter."

Duchess Cordelia sat beside Mr. Jackson. "What matter?"

Mrs. Jackson was about to speak, but Mr. Jackson held up a hand. "You must promise to tell no one —"

Ah, Mrs. Jackson thought. That would be like telling the wind not to blow.

"— but the police believe that the Head Valet was murdered!"

Duchess Cordelia gasped, pressing her lined hands to her mouth. "Goodness!" She leaned forward, glancing around. "Do you think we're in any danger?"

"Surely not," Mr. Jackson said. "But who would want to murder him? He seemed a decent enough chap."

Mrs. Jackson snorted quietly, amused.

Yet his words seemed to draw some recollection from the dowager, who leaned forward to speak in hushed tones. "Did you know that he was an awful flirt? With married women, no less!" She leaned back. "One of the husbands, that's who I'd put my money on." She gave a self-satisfied nod. But then her face turned sad. "Poor Effie —"

Mrs. Jackson said, "Why Effie?"

"Oh, my dear ... you really must not mention it. But she got entangled with the man. He broke her heart some time back, and I believe she still carries a torch for him." The old woman's head drooped as she shook it sorrowfully. "She looks cheery enough, but when she thinks no one's looking ..."

"What a pity." Mr. Jackson seemed to truly mean it.

This brought back uncomfortable memories of herself becoming entangled with the wrong man, which Mrs. Jackson pushed aside. "Do you know who any of these husbands might be?"

Duchess Cordelia gained a new energy. "I shall write you a list. It will probably not be complete, but —"

Mr. Jackson chuckled. "Why in the world a list?"

"Hush, dear," Mrs. Jackson said, not wanting him to dissuade the woman when she'd finally given them something useful. "A list would be lovely."

"Well," Duchess Cordelia said, "I know you're investigators. I was going to ask Mrs. Jackson to the library with me, but I saw our Mr. Carlo hurry over to speak with you. And of course everyone knows Mr. Vincenzo is Mr. Carlo's cousin, and so —"

Mr. Jackson said, "You really are remarkable."

Duchess Cordelia blushed, giving him a shy smile. "Why, thank you, sir."

Mrs. Jackson chuckled, amused. "Your list would be ever so helpful."

The waiter brought Duchess Cordelia's meal to her.

"I do hope so," she said, in between bites. "My main hope is that the culprit is someone from outside the Hotel. We've had enough scandal here to last a lifetime."

***

After their plates were taken away, Mr. Jackson asked for pen and paper so Duchess Cordelia might write. As she wrote, the waiters cleared the huge dining room, removing the plates, the silverware, the centerpieces, the tablecloths. Maids with vacuum cleaners began working over the carpeting.

Had Mr. Carlo been aware of what his cousin was up to?

Perhaps he didn't want to see what everyone around him did, Mr. Jackson thought. He'd had this experience himself, in other matters.

Duchess Cordelia hesitated for just a moment, wrote one more name, then set the pen down with a smack. "There! You have learned all I know on the topic."

"You have our sincere thanks," he said.

"This will be ever so helpful," said his wife.

The dowager beamed. "You simply must tell me all about it when you catch the man."

He could feel his wife withdraw into herself. "These matters are confidential. Imagine if we'd told everyone about what happened the last time the Hotel had this sort of thing go on."

"Oh," Duchess Cordelia said, seeming dismayed.

"You see," his wife continued, "some things are best left silent."

Mr. Jackson heartily agreed. "Never fear, my Lady, you'll learn who did the deed soon enough." He took the paper from her and glanced quickly over it: relatively small print, both sides. "Assuming we can."

Bessie began pawing at his leg, and he smiled down at her. "Ready to go outside again?"

***

Mrs. Jackson held onto Mr. Jackson's arm as the couple strolled down Lake Shore Drive with Bessie, looking at the shops.

They'd not been out much the first time they'd been here, what with her injury and all. Then after they'd solved the unpleasantness at the Hotel, her Mr. Jackson had been focused on seeing the sights. Duchess Cordelia, of course, had wanted them to see "everything."

That made her giggle.

"What amuses you?"

Mrs. Jackson smiled to herself. "Just thinking of our Duchess. She does so love this place."

"Ah," he said. "Then you were thinking of our last visit here."

He did that on relatively little information. She took his hand. "You know, you're quite remarkable yourself."

She loved to see his blush, his little smile.

The she realized the truth: she was becoming fond of him. She was becoming enamored.

And it frightened her.

When she agreed to marry him, she'd been fleeing the devastation of her past life. His offer seemed for the best, but she only accepted because she didn't think it anything other than a suitable arrangement.

They'd been bitter rivals for over a decade. She knew of his fondness for men. And while recently he'd been more congenial, she'd thought him to be such a scoundrel that she didn't care if he died, as everyone else had who she'd let into her life.

And as he'd said: *it might make life easier for you*.

But then it turned out he'd been in love with her.

She squeezed his arm tightly. "You must take care. We mustn't be seen to have too much interest in police matters, not so close to the Hotel."

He smiled to himself. "My dear girl. You worry yourself far too much. We have Sergeant Nestor, and Mr. Carlo, and a host of others here who'll protect us." Then he turned to face her, people streaming back and forth around them. "Not to mention my men."

She'd forgotten about them.

He took her hands. "So you see, we shall be just fine." He offered his arm, and they continued to stroll along. "There's not a man in the world who can hurt us."

9

The couple took tea in their rooms. Mr. Jackson sat with his wife reading the books they'd gotten from the library earlier, until Mr. Raymond came to dress him for dinner.

Mr. Raymond examined the blemishes on his neck closely. "Your skin seems to still be agitating itself there." He drew back, hand to his chin. "It's strange: usually letting the hair grow does the trick."

He went to the bathroom to wash his hands, leaving the water running. When he returned, he opened his kit. "I'll do another heat treatment after the ointment, to open the pores. That will help drive the medication in."

Mr. Jackson nodded. Despite still feeling uneasy about him for some reason, the man seemed most competent. And quite sanitary. "Sounds good."

Mr. Jackson watched as Mr. Raymond prepared to work. The man had a medium build, but his arms strained the shirt he wore, particularly when he did his mixing. "You look like a man who values his exercise."

Mr. Raymond grinned. "I've done a fair amount in my time. But I had to help after my father died."

"I'm sorry to hear about it."

Mr. Raymond shrugged, glancing away, and spoke lightly. "No matter. He died when I was a boy."

A boy? Mr. Jackson recalled when his own father died. Even as a grown man, it'd been painful. "That must have been difficult."

Mr. Raymond began applying the ointment. "Yeah, well, that was life. I started sweeping for the neighbor's shop, then when I got old enough, I worked as a messenger boy. Then later on, I took up boxing."

"Boxing? You managed not to get hit too badly."

Mr. Raymond let out a laugh. "Got my nose broke once. The doctor who fixed me said I should get out before I got concussed, or worse. I signed up for valet training at his advice."

"That was quite kind of him."

He seemed surprised. "Never thought of it that way. It did come in handy: during the war, only those with valet training got to tend the officers."

"How was the training?"

Mr. Raymond shrugged. "Hard at first. I didn't have the schooling that some did. But I like it."

He went into the bathroom, turned off the water, then returned with a steaming towel. "I still do the boxer training on the side. And I particularly like the lifting of weights. It relaxes me."

The hot, moist towel on Mr. Jackson's face seemed quite relaxing. He looked forward to dinner with the Neubergs tonight. Their dinner upon the yacht six days earlier seemed a century past. "Say, would you care for dinner with us sometime?"

Mr. Raymond's eyes widened. "That's very much appreciated, sir! But fraternizing with clients isn't allowed. Company policy. I wouldn't have gone to play dominoes if I'd have known you'd be there."

"Well, I don't want you in trouble. But I don't want you not to play alongside your sister on our account. Would it be all right if we stayed at separate tables?"

Mr. Raymond considered this. "I'll ask, sir. I don't see why not."

Some time later, Mr. Jackson met George Neuberg and his parents in the lobby. He felt pleased to see them, particularly George, who he hadn't gotten a chance to speak with since the dominoes game.

George looked more rested, back to his old self, and his parents seemed well. But when they met in the lobby, Bessie barked at Mr. Neuberg until Mrs. Jackson brought the dog away to be watched during dinner.

As she left, Mr. Jackson turned to the Neubergs. "I'm terribly sorry; I don't know what's come over her."

Mr. Neuberg shrugged. "Dogs don't seem to like me, and I have no idea why."

That amused Mr. Jackson. "Who knows what might go on in the mind of a dog?"

"True," Mr. Neuberg said. "Say, I like the beard. It suits you."

"Thanks." Mr. Jackson wasn't so fond of it. If only his skin would heal so he might have a proper shave!

Mrs. Jackson walked up. "She's all settled in with her dinner. They said to take as long as we like."

"Well done," Mr. Jackson said. Then he turned to his guests. "Come, our table's waiting."

It'd been a good idea to reserve the table: not an empty seat remained save for the ones around theirs.

George gave Will a bemused grin when the waiter showed up to take their order.

"Well, aren't we spiffy," Will said to George, then nudged him. "Out with the big cheese, are we?"

George said, "These are my parents."

"Oh." Will rushed to slide in Mr. Neuberg's chair, then Mr. Jackson's, then George's, who for some reason had placed himself directly across the table. "No harm meant, sir."

George laughed. "Don't 'sir' me, ya whisk broom, get us our menus."

"Right away." Will went off, feeling his chin. There really wasn't much there, but he'd evidently forgotten to shave before dinner.

"Your dining room is spectacular," Mrs. Neuberg said. "And your friends seem very nice."

George smiled to himself.

Will came back with the menus and began passing them around.

Mr. Jackson said, "Order whatever you like; the food is magnificent."

George said, "But —"

Mr. Jackson raised his hand. "I insist. I invited you. It's only fair."

George's eyes narrowed, but he said nothing further.

What could possibly be bothering him? Mr. Jackson resolved to speak to him about it later.

But the conversation and the food pushed it out of his mind, and it wasn't until he lay in bed that evening that he remembered. Oh, well, he thought. I'll have plenty of chance to speak to him about it later.

***

The next day at lunch, Mrs. Jackson made sure to sit facing the dining room door. She generally did as a matter of course — an investigator would never want someone to approach from behind unseen.

But today, she felt all a-flutter.

Would Miss Ophelia attend? Would she and Mr. Jackson get along? Would Bessie like her?

"I've never seen you so unsettled," Mr. Jackson said, yet in a good-natured way. He took her left hand. "I'm sure all will go well."

The table was almost full, their choice made on purpose so as not to have the conversation occupied too much by the old dowager's reminiscing.

Miss Ophelia Denton appeared then, and was shown to their table. Mrs. Jackson rose. "Come round and sit here."

Bessie, who'd been lying on the floor beside Mrs. Jackson's chair, perked up her ears.

"Mr. Hector Jackson," Mrs. Jackson said, "may I introduce Miss Ophelia Denton."

Ophelia held out her hand. "A pleasure, sir."

Mr. Jackson said, "My wife has told me much about you." He gestured down. "And this is Bessie."

"Hello, Bessie," Ophelia said.

Bessie's eyes were bright, her tail wagging.

They sat and placed their orders. A waiter poured their tea.

"This hotel is lovely," Ophelia said. "I've passed it for years now, but never dared step inside."

"Oh! You must see the entirety," Mrs. Jackson said, then felt foolish. She sounded like Duchess Cordelia!

Ophelia gave her a wry smile. "The grand tour? I'd not miss that."

Mr. Jackson said, "What is it you do, Miss Denton? To pass by our hotel every day."

Ophelia grinned. "Oh, I'm a dancer over at Club Patruni." She leaned back. "Don't suppose you folks have ever heard of it."

Mrs. Jackson shook her head, glanced at Mr. Jackson, who shrugged. Then she turned back to Ophelia. "Do you like it there?"

It was Ophelia's turn to shrug. "I don't have to cook and I don't have to clean. I stay on stage, so no flippers on the fanny. And I don't have to muck about with children." She grinned. "Suits me just fine."

The mention of children sparked a pang in Mrs. Jackson's chest. She missed her little son terribly. How she wished things might have gone differently!

But she had to accept it: he was gone. She could never see him, never hold him again.

Mr. Jackson's hand grasped hers. "My wife's in mourning for her child."

Ophelia grimaced. "I'm so very sorry. I had no idea!" Her hand was soft, holding hers. Then she opened her napkin. "We'll not speak on the topic again."

That made Mrs. Jackson smile a bit. "You know, I think we might get along just fine."

They fell silent, yet it didn't feel awkward the way such silences often do.

Mrs. Jackson felt interested in Ophelia's work. "What's the Club Patruni like?"

"Fun place," Ophelia said. "Ground floor's got dinner and a regular show. But there's this area downstairs —"

"Ah," Mr. Jackson said, as if now he understood everything. "You work there."

"Yeah," Ophelia said, her tone approving. "You know your onions, don't ya?"

Mr. Jackson grinned.

The waiters set down their plates. Mrs. Jackson got the gist of the conversation, but the talk here was still strange to her. "What kind of dancing do you do?"

Ophelia gave her a wink and a grin. "You'll have to come by and see."

Mr. Jackson stirred. "So what does your mother think of —"

At the word "mother," Ophelia's face fell.

"Oh, dear," Mr. Jackson said. "Forgive me."

Ophelia didn't look at either of them. "What the war didn't get, the flu did." She raised her head, squaring her shoulders. "I like to think she'd want me happy." She turned to face her food. "You gotta live life today is my motto. Tomorrow's just a word, not a guarantee."

Mr. Jackson nodded. "Well said."

Ophelia picked up her fork. "Don't know about you, but I'm hungry."

Mr. Jackson laughed, then unfurled his cloth napkin, setting it on his lap.

Mrs. Jackson began poking at her food. *You gotta live life today.*

She wasn't entirely sure she knew how.

***

It turned out that Miss Denton had the day off. So after they'd eaten, Mr. Jackson proposed a tour of the Hotel.

The three of them walked the gardens, peered at the spa area, looked out over the docks. They even climbed the grand staircase and walked round looking at the sights there. But Miss Denton seemed most fascinated by the elevators.

After a few rides up and down, Mr. Jackson said, "There's another swimming pool and garden on the roof. If you'd like join us, we could have tea there. Or we could have it brought to our suite instead."

"Is it that late?" Miss Denton seemed surprised at the time, rather than worried about having somewhere to be. "Let's see your suite."

She gasped in delight at their parlor. "It's gorgeous!" Rushing to the parlor's French doors, she flung them open and stepped upon the balcony. "And the view!"

Mr. Jackson went to the telephone in the corner.

"Room Service, may I assist you?"

"Full tea service to 3205, the parlor door."

"Right away, sir."

He went out to the balcony.

Miss Denton said, "— and the fellow had snuck his way right under the costume rack! Oh, you should have seen his face when the bouncers arrived."

His wife laughed, the sun on her face, her hair flowing free.

How fortunate I am, he thought.

She glanced over at him with a happy smile, her cheeks coloring, and he thought his heart might seize up within him. *She's so beautiful*.

A movement out of the corner of his eye. Miss Denton looked between them, her face guarded.

He smiled at her. For an instant, he felt moved. "It's good for my wife to have friends here."

The girl's delightfully wry smile returned. "Do you not have many friends here?"

His wife gave a one-shoulder shrug. "Acquaintances, many. Friends?" She glanced at him, took his hand. "I suppose our dowager Duchess is friendly to us."

Miss Denton's eyes widened. "A Duchess? Here?"

He said, "She lives down the hall. We made her acquaintance the last time we stayed."

His wife grinned. "She's a lovely old lady. I'll introduce you. But she'll talk your ear off if you let her."

The parlor door bell rang. "Ah," Mr. Jackson said, "tea's here." He went to the door, Bessie following. To his surprise, George stood there! "Come in!"

George chuckled. "Didn't expect me here, did you?"

"Not at all."

He wheeled the cart into the room. "They've got us rotating jobs. Want it set up on the table there?"

"Certainly." Mr. Jackson said.

The two women came into the room. His wife said, "George! You must meet our new friend. This is Miss Ophelia Denton." She then gestured to George. "George Neuberg and my Mr. Jackson are dear friends."

A wry smile. "Are you now?" Miss Denton held out her hand. "Pleasure to meet ya."

The four of them got the table set up, Bessie sniffing the cart and whining. George laughed. "This goes much faster with four!"

"Sit with us for a bit, then," Mr. Jackson said, "since you have the extra time."

George grinned. "I do believe I will."

Miss Denton looked between himself and George, more than a bit puzzled, it seemed, at the sight of a waiter sitting with Hotel guests.

Mr. Jackson said to George, "How did your parents like dinner last night?"

George's easy attitude disappeared. "They enjoyed it very much. They asked me to offer their thanks."

What was wrong? "Think nothing of it! They've hosted us more than once. It was my pleasure."

George rose. "I best be off, before they send someone looking." He nodded to Miss Denton. "A pleasure to meet you." Then he took the cart and left.

Miss Denton said, "You've got interesting friends."

Mr. Jackson said, "I suppose we do." But his mind was on George. He'd been acting odd last night at dinner, too.

Perhaps he'd had an argument with his parents. His father could be overbearing, his mother, clingy. It would irritate any man after too long.

His wife and Miss Denton were eating, drinking tea, and chatting. Bessie seemed intent upon a couple of sandwiches his wife had emptied onto a saucer.

Miss Denton looked over at him. "So if you don't mind me asking, what was all that business in the alley about, anyway?"

He and his wife exchanged a glance, and he recalled her words to Duchess Cordelia. "I don't think we should say, not now."

His wife gave him an amused smile. "A man was attacked. We're still trying to figure out who did it."

Miss Denton's eyes widened. "Attacked? Next to this rich hotel?" She sounded dismayed. "Right near where I walk every day!"

His wife looked chagrined. "I didn't consider that."

Miss Denton smiled at her. "Never fear, I always stay to public roads. No alleys for me!"

It turned out that Miss Denton lived in a boarding house not too far off. "It's not bad. Room and board with a bath down the hall."

His wife said, "That sounds near where that old lady died a few months back."

"I knew your dog looked familiar," Miss Denton said. "It was right next door. This little gal used to follow me along the fence when I'd go off to work." She smiled under the table. "Fancy meeting you here!"

Bessie looked up, wagging her tail, then set back upon her meal.

The dog had an unusually good appetite these days. But she didn't seem to be getting any bigger. At least, not that he could see.

Perhaps it's some instinct, he thought. He'd heard that animals sensed the coming of winter.

His reverie was broken as Miss Denton rose. He scrambled to his feet. "Must you go?"

She chuckled. "If I don't show up for dinner on my days off, my landlady'll toss me out."

"Well, we don't want that," Mr. Jackson said, amused. "Let's be away then. I'll call down for a taxi."

"That's not necessary," Miss Denton said. "It's really not far."

"I insist," he said. The sky was beginning to darken. "I'll not have you out walking at night, and that's final."

As he went to telephone, Miss Denton said to his wife, "Guess I better not tell Grandpa my last show ends at two A.M."

His wife giggled. Giggled!

Grandpa? Good grief, he thought. I'm only thirty-three. "Yes," he said into the telephone, "a taxi. We'll be down in five minutes."

As they waited for the elevator, his wife said, "Would you like to play dominoes with us later tonight?"

Miss Denton tipped her head to the side a bit. "Never played." She shrugged. "Wouldn't know how."

He said, "Neither of us had played before last week's game. And you can meet Duchess Cordelia. We play in her suite."

Miss Denton hesitated, eyes wide. Then she smiled in a devil-may-care fashion. "Why not?"

His wife said, "It's after dinner. Around ten?"

"I'll meet you in the lobby at half past nine," Miss Denton said. "Unless you want to tell me the number."

The elevator door opened. He said, "We'll be happy to meet you down there. I'll send a taxi for you." He felt amused at the puzzled expression that crossed the girl's face, then her slow nod as she figured it all out. "It's settled then."

After they put Miss Denton into a cab and sent her on her way, his wife took his arm. "Thank you for being so kind to her."

He felt moved, so much so that they were back into the lobby before he might speak. "You've been very kind to George as well."

She gave a little pleased-with-herself smile and squeezed his arm. "We all need friends here."

They'd reached the elevator. "Indeed we do." The elevator opened and they went in. "Thirty-two, please."

The man at the controls nodded. "Yes, sir."

The couple stood in silence as the elevator moved upward. Right before they reached their floor, his wife said, "I wonder what friends our man had."

"It's a fair question."

***

When the couple returned to their parlor and the door firmly shut, Mrs. Jackson let Bessie off her leash to sniff about once more.

Yet Mr. Jackson stood in the center of the room.

She said, "What is it?"

"If Mr. Earl Vincenzo had offended someone so mortally as to have them kill him this way, wouldn't he know? Why would he ruin his shoes, as you put it, to meet up with someone in an alley, alone, that he knew wanted him dead?"

She had no idea.

"And in broad daylight, too? Nothing about this is making sense."

"It feels personal," she said. "Why not shoot the man? To hit him on the head ... go to all the work of putting him into the sewers —"

A look of horror crossed his face. "Mr. Vincenzo had to have helped dig out the manhole cover. Or at least be standing there when they did so."

"What do you mean?"

"Just picture it. Mr. Vincenzo goes down the alley. Moments later, the other valet almost hits a truck going in after him. So we have the head valet and the truck in the alley. Am I right?"

"I suppose."

"So whoever is driving the truck — let's say our two men — get out and talk to the valet. Now, the alley is still covered in gravel."

She nodded. "So they were there for some time."

"Yes. But they had plenty to spare. I'll wager if we find another witness, they'll merely say they saw the truck parked there. And if they passed on the other end, all they'd see were men and a truck. And even if they saw the murder take place, it'd be difficult for someone standing a full block away to identify them, not unless they knew them well."

Realization dawned. "They had to have parked behind the manhole! So there must be some way to mark its location that we missed."

"Very true! Well done. So the men are there. Perhaps the Head Valet believes there's something under there that he wants."

She recalled the way the gravel had crunched and slipped as they walked through it. "Important enough for him to ruin his shoes over."

He chuckled. "Indeed." Then his mirth faded. "But the callousness of those men! All that time, knowing the Head Valet's fate, yet allowing him to stand there."

She pictured the scene. "Or worse, help perform his own death."

Mr. Jackson nodded.

"So we look for at least two shovels," she said. "One is sure to be what hit him."

"You think so?"

She shrugged. "Seems reasonable. If you're going to hit someone after digging, and you both need to dig, you won't come up to them carrying a gun."

He seemed to gain a new energy. "I'll speak with the manager tomorrow about the shovels. Care to join me?"

She shook her head. She didn't like it. She didn't want to do it. But she now knew what she had to do. "Perhaps I **will** speak with the man's wife. She would know of his friends. And who hated him so fiercely."

10

The next day, Mrs. Jackson left Bessie with the veterinarian's boys and took a taxi to the Head Valet's home, arriving precisely at eleven. "Wait here, if you please," she said to the driver. "I shouldn't be long."

Mrs. Vincenzo lived in an area far too rich for the salary of a valet, even the Head Valet of a hotel so grand as the Myriad. A maid answered the door, ushering Mrs. Jackson to a spacious parlor. "She'll be right with you."

Mrs. Vincenzo was a tall, elegant woman, perhaps forty, with long black hair done up into a swirling bun reminiscent of days past. She took Mrs. Jackson's hand briefly then sat on a chair across the gilt-edged coffee table. "Thank you for visiting, ma'am. I admit to being surprised by your call."

"My husband and I are helping Mr. Carlo learn who hurt your husband," Mrs. Jackson said. "But I did want to express our condolences as well."

"Thank you," she said. Then her head drooped as she looked away. "How may I help you?"

"I know the police have asked these things," Mrs. Jackson said. "But perhaps you might have recalled something since then. Would anyone have reason to harm your husband?"

"Many have such reason." Mrs. Vincenzo let out a small amused snort, lips curling up at the corners. "I suppose I'm a suspect, even."

"You?"

She breathed deeply: in, then out. "My husband could be a violent man when provoked. And I seemed to ever provoke him. But I didn't do it."

"No one thinks you did," Mrs. Jackson said gently. "We'd like to learn who might have, though."

Mrs. Vincenzo nodded slowly. "I have a fear —"

At the way the woman stopped so suddenly, Mrs. Jackson felt a chill. "Of what?"

The words seemed ripped from Mrs. Vincenzo. "Let it not be!" She pressed her hands to her face.

Mrs. Jackson leaned forward. "What is it you fear?"

"My father. Could he have done this?"

Mrs. Jackson leaned back, mind whirling. Of course, she thought. What man wouldn't do anything to protect his daughter? And this had to be why she didn't want to speak with the police.

"Oh, that I'd said nothing, showed him no injuries, made no complaint! He's threatened to kill my husband more than once." The woman dropped her hands; tears lay on her face. "To lose my husband and father both!"

"We don't know anything yet. Could he do this?"

"I don't know!" Mrs.Vincenzo seemed despondent. "Which is worse? To know the fact of his good or bad, or to doubt him? My own father!" She began weeping.

Mrs. Jackson sat beside her, rested her hand upon Mrs. Vincenzo's back. "I'm glad you told me. Now we can clear your mind once and for all. My husband and I will learn the truth."

Mrs. Vincenzo wiped her eyes. "Thank you."

"And your father's name is?"

"Oh, yes, forgive me. Leo Trappola."

Mrs. Jackson retrieved a pad and pencil from her handbag and wrote the name down. Then she recalled what Ophelia had said, and decided to take a different tack. "Did your husband have many friends? Or people your children —?"

She shrugged. "We have no children. We lived separate lives. If he had friends, I knew nothing of it."

"He never mentioned anyone? No one came over?"

Her face pinched in concentration. "There was some tradesman who came by a few weeks back. They talked in here. An older man."

"Do you recall his name?"

She hesitated. "Newman? Newport?"

A chill ran down Mrs. Jackson's back. "Neuberg?"

"Yes, that's the name. I'm sure of it."

Oh, dear, she thought. "You said many people had reason to wish your husband harm. Who else?"

Mrs.Vincenzo peered at her hands. "He's not been a good man, Mrs. Jackson. Even from his youth." She sighed. "When I first met him, he was what the kids these days call a hoodlum. I was young and stupidly in love, but even then, I should have known he'd meet an untimely end."

"Was he with the Mob?"

She shrugged. "Not any of the bigger groups. But yes, though he tried to keep me from knowing. And of course, now he's working with Monty, who's always into something. Earl told me once not long ago that he wanted to get his life right —" at this, she shook her head. "Now I suppose I'll never know for sure."

"But you don't know the specifics? What gang?"

She shook her head. "I'd tell you if I did, I swear."

Even after all he'd done, she still loved him. Mrs. Jackson put her hand upon Mrs. Vincenzo's, feeling a surge of grief. "I'm ever so sorry for your loss."

On the way home, Mrs. Jackson considered the matter. Why would George's father come here? Surely he didn't have anything to do with a murder. Did he?

Bessie didn't like him. But that didn't mean he was a murderer. What possible motive might he have?

And though she felt Mr. Leo Trappola to be a likely suspect, something about the idea of either one being involved bothered her. The Chicago waterfront was wide, the countryside vast. Why kill Mr. Vincenzo in the middle of the city, risking discovery?

And there were much easier ways to dispose of a body. Shoveling gravel and hoisting manholes at noon seemed a bit much for men who had to be at least sixty.

Could either one have hired others to do it?

First things first, she thought. She didn't even know Mr. Neuberg's line of work.

She decided to begin there. The man could have a perfectly reasonable explanation for visiting.

Then there was the other matter.

Mrs. Jackson let out a sigh. She'd worked as a private investigator for many years. But the thought of tracking down Mr. Leo Trappola made her weary.

I'm too old for this.

Sergeant Nestor wanted her to get information from this woman, and she'd done it. Next time she saw him, she'd pass it along and see what he thought. For all she knew, he might already have spoken to the man.

She chuckled softly to herself as she got out of the taxi in front of the Hotel. At least now old Nestor had to admit she was useful.

***

Earlier that morning, Mr. Jackson had put on his scuffed shoes before accompanying his wife downstairs. When they parted in the lobby, Mr. Jackson stood for a moment watching the enormous fountain in the center there. He felt as if pieces were still missing to this puzzle they'd been handed. But what?

No answer appearing, he went to see the manager, who left to investigate whether shovels were missing.

In the lobby once more, Mr. Jackson still had no ideas arise. So he decided to look at the alley.

The way was entirely bare. A few police stood at each end of it, but apparently Sergeant Nestor had told them about him, because they allowed him to pass.

Mr. Jackson stood ten feet from the open manhole. No marks stood on the walls beside it, nor anywhere along the route from the street.

Mr. Jackson approached a uniformed officer, a pale young man with big ears and freckles. "Were there any objects found in the alleyway?"

The officer blinked, shaking his head. "Don't rightly know. Forensics would have all that."

Mr. Jackson nodded. "Thank you, sir."

The officer nodded. "I seen you before, that night the waiter got sick. I was keeping the swells out the crime scene. You the house dick now?"

"I beg your pardon?"

"The hotel detective."

Mr. Jackson felt surprised at the idea. "I hadn't considered the matter."

The young officer chuckled. "Is Carlo at least paying you to come out here?"

Mr. Jackson considered the fact that he and his wife had lived in this magnificent hotel twice now, and so far, for free. "In a sense, yes!"

The officer grinned. "Then good for you."

Mr. Jackson fetched Bessie from the veterinarian's boys, who'd been playing with her, and returned to his suite. His wife was still with Mrs. Vincenzo, so he took off his scuffed-up shoes and stretched out on his bed.

Bessie began sniffing every bit of the room, as usual.

He let out a weary sigh. His wife was so incredibly brave to meet with that woman, after all she'd been through. Even though he didn't know the details of what happened the night before they'd married, he knew enough. She'd been hurt terribly, more in her heart than even that huge scar upon her arm, and he had to think of a way to help her recover.

He felt relieved that she and Miss Denton were getting along. From what he'd seen so far, this girl would provide quite a bit of diversion on her own.

The rash under his beard still felt tender. If anything, it seemed to be getting worse. He'd never had such an extensive rash before, not even as a boy.

Could it be something he ate? They'd eaten well on the steamer, but this new Chef's cooking was quite rich. He'd heard of people reacting in this way to new foods, although it'd never happened to him.

He patted his belly, which he'd let go a bit. Maybe he needed to start keeping better watch over his diet. And getting more exercise as well.

He sat up. "Here, Bessie, let's go for a walk."

They took the elevator down to the main floor, but instead of going to the right and out to the lobby, Mr. Jackson decided to turn left, past the veterinary and the gardens, then left again to the hallway from the kitchens to the platform out back.

George stood leaning against the wall outside the kitchens, tying his shoe. He glanced up. "What are you doing here?"

"Just walking about." He went to George. "Is everything okay?"

George glanced away. "Fine. Did your friend enjoy the day?"

For a moment, Mr. Jackson was at a loss. "Oh, the girl. Yes, Miss Denton had a grand time. Stayed almost to dinner."

George raised his eyebrows.

Mr. Jackson chuckled. "She's lively, that one. Be good for my wife to have someone closer to her age than Duchess Cordelia to spend time with."

George nodded slowly.

"Say," Mr. Jackson said, "do you want to see Miss Denton's show? I was thinking the three of us could have dinner there."

"Don't you want to play dominoes tonight?"

"Good grief. I completely forgot. Tomorrow, then?"

"You're lucky I'm scheduled early. Where at?"

Then Mr. Jackson had to recall. "Club Patruni?"

George laughed. "It's been a while since I've been **there**. Sure, I think I can swing it."

"Let's meet in the lobby tomorrow night at seven."

***

When Mrs. Jackson's taxi pulled up to the Hotel, Mr. Jackson and little Bessie were there, walking along past the doors. She paid the driver as Harry opened the door for her.

Her Mr. Jackson glanced back, reversing course to meet her. He kissed her cheek. "Did it go well?"

"Well enough. What have you been up to?"

"This and that. Took our Queen Bess for a stroll. Want to have lunch here?"

"Let's go up to the suite first: I need to freshen up."

So the couple took the elevator to their floor.

Effie's maid cart was outside their suite, the parlor door open.

Mrs. Jackson knocked.

Effie's voice emerged from Mr. Jackson's bedroom. "Come in."

Mrs. Jackson turned to him. "I'll just be a moment."

After combing out her hair and other such matters, she returned to find Effie plumping the sofa cushions in the parlor. "There! All done," Effie said.

"You do a marvelous job," Mrs. Jackson said.

"Thank you, ma'am."

"You seem in good spirits today. What news?"

Effie blushed. She glanced around, lowering her voice. "I've been proposed to."

"Congratulations." Mrs. Jackson kept her voice low also. "Who's the lucky fellow?"

She beamed. "Mr. Clifton Strait. The Headwaiter."

Why would she want to hide her happiness? "Do you have a date planned?"

She hesitated. "I've not answered yet."

Mrs. Jackson said, "I see." A quick glance at the door: Mr. Jackson stood out in the hall still, turned away.

"I want to marry him, ma'am," Effie said, "truly." She bit her lip. "We just need some discussion first."

"Hmm." Mrs. Jackson entirely understood. But she'd kept far too many secrets in her day. "If you trust this man, if you truly love him, tell him every bit. If you don't, walk away and don't look back."

Effie's eyes widened. Then she nodded.

Mrs. Jackson smiled at her. "Either way, your conscience will be clear. Believe me: it's the best way to live." Her conscience was entirely clear, and had been so for some time. Every secret she'd ever had was revealed in public, long ago. She hoped no woman would ever have to go through that.

Effie peered downward for a moment. Then her head rose. "I will, ma'am, thank you."

Mrs. Jackson raised her voice then. "Let me know how it all turns out."

After Effie left, Mrs. Jackson let Bessie loose to inspect matters.

Mr. Jackson said, "What was all that about?"

She gave him a grin and a giggle. "Didn't your mother tell you not to pry?"

He let out a little "hmph". Then he laughed. "My mother told me quite a few things, most of which I ignored. Keep your secret, then."

"It's not my secret to tell." Yet she considered the conversation she'd just had with the woman. Could

Effie's hesitation to accept the Headwaiter's proposal be due to not wanting to reveal her prior entanglement with the Head Valet?

But if the man already knew of it ... the timing of his offer was much too much of a coincidence. "Suppose a man's death put you at an advantage. Would that not make you a suspect?"

"I'd say it would."

Mrs. Jackson nodded to herself. Yet to reveal it now, just after Effie confided in her ... if the man were innocent, it would be dreadful for them both. "Too many people benefited from Mr. Vincenzo's death. It's a wonder the man lived as long as he did."

11

That evening, as usual, Mr. Jackson's valet arrived to dress him for dinner. After examining the skin under his beard, though, the valet proposed a more intensive treatment.

Mr. Jackson lay on his bed propped up by many pillows, a hot towel covering his beard. "How long have you worked here?"

Mr. Raymond stood by a small folding table, mixing something in a cup. "Off and on for a little over a year. Just luck of the draw where you're sent."

"I didn't realize."

"Yes, sir."

"Your sister works here. Do you get to know the people here much?"

Mr. Raymond began to whip the cup's contents. "Just who I meet here and there." He gave a quick glance over. "That night you were there was my first night at dominoes, too."

Mr. Jackson felt pleased. "Well, fancy that!"

Mr. Raymond took the towel off and began applying whatever was in the cup to Mr. Jackson's face, massaging it in. "This should help strengthen the skin."

Having his face massaged felt pleasant. After the massage was completed and another hot towel applied, Mr. Jackson said, "We plan to stay for a little while."

"I'm sure Effie will be glad for that, sir. She's fond of you both."

Mr. Jackson smiled to himself. "But it doesn't feel right to live somewhere and not know the names of your staff. I've gotten to meet some of the back men so far, but not any of the drivers. Do you know them?"

His valet tensed up, just a bit. "Yeah, a couple. Here, come sit in the chair and I'll do a comb-out and trim."

Mr. Jackson moved to the chair. "Forgive me; I don't mean to pry."

Mr. Raymond focused on his combing, then brought out the scissors and began snipping. "Well, the two I know are the ones being talked about. For that murder."

"I see."

"I don't want to get mixed up in any of it."

Mr. Jackson couldn't blame him. Yet it seemed Mr. Raymond might already be mixed up in it, if what Duchess Cordelia had told him of the closeness between his sister and the dead man were true. "I don't blame you: it must be horrible for everyone."

Mr. Raymond moved to the other side of the chair, eyes downcast. "It has been."

Mr. Jackson felt sorry for the man. His sister must be going through a multitude of feelings about the man's death. And who wouldn't want to comfort and protect their sister? "Cheer up; things will improve, I feel certain of it."

***

That night after dinner, Duchess Cordelia's suite overflowed with players, so much so that she had to call for extra tables. The Headwaiter was there, a powerfully built man who resembled the Head Valet. Ophelia was there, as was George.

The dowager insisted the couple sit with her, and to round out the table she invited Will to sit with them also.

Mrs. Jackson glanced over at the next table. Effie seemed as much in conversation with the Headwaiter as she was attending to her tiles. Her brother Stanley sat beside her, looking glum.

"So many here tonight!" Duchess Cordelia set a tile. "If this keeps up, I'll have to order another box!"

Mr. Jackson laid a double. "Nice problem to have."

The way he smiled to himself made Mrs. Jackson think he had an idea brewing.

Duchess Cordelia beamed, raising her voice a bit. "I do so love having everyone here. It gives me something to look forward to."

At the break, the others drifted off to eat, drink, and so on. Mr. Jackson said, "Miss Denton, we'd like to visit sometime. Is there anything we should know?"

Ophelia blushed all the way to her hairline. "You sure you want to do that?"

Mr. Jackson said, "We're sure."

"Then don't go in the front. Come round to the side door and knock three times. When they open up, tell them you're friends with Carrie."

Mrs. Jackson said, "Carrie?"

"Yeah. That's the code this month. If they ask, say you just met."

Mr. Jackson grinned. "Got it."

"You really want to see me?"

Mrs. Jackson said, "Of course we do."

Mr. Jackson excused himself, and Ophelia said she was getting a drink.

Mrs. Jackson found George off in a corner, eating a large sandwich. "May I join you?"

George gestured to a chair beside him.

She could sure use a cigarette. But she didn't know whether the dowager allowed smoking in her suite.

"What can I do for you?"

Mrs. Jackson smiled. "Nothing, really. But I was wondering. Your father seems quite wealthy. What does he do?"

George nodded as he chewed. Then he swallowed. "Builds boats. Our family business, really. He took over from my grandpa, who took over from his." He shrugged. "I grew up on boats as much as on land, now that I think of it."

"Does he buy boats as well?"

George set his sandwich down. "Sometimes. Why?"

"I learned something curious about your father today, that's all. He visited Mr. Vincenzo's home a few weeks back."

"Why is that curious?"

"Because according to his wife, your Head Valet didn't get many visitors."

George nodded soberly. "Is my father a suspect?"

Mrs. Jackson shrugged. "Not really."

George snorted. "I should hope not. My father's a forceful, strong-willed man, but he faints dead away at the sight of blood."

"That must have made for an interesting childhood."

"I learned to go to my mother after a tussle if I wanted tending."

"Rather than having to tend to him."

George let out a laugh. "Yeah."

***

They were at Duchess Cordelia's until late. The next morning, the couple decided to have breakfast in their rooms. As they ate, Mrs. Jackson said, "When I spoke with Ophelia, back when I followed her, she mentioned something strange."

"Oh?"

"Well, the brochure at the front desk clearly showed large cobblestones in that alley. And she mentioned a time when the alley was cobbles rather than gravel. But she mentioned it in a way which makes me think that there's more to it."

Mr. Jackson leaned back, coffee in hand. "Why put gravel over perfectly good cobblestones?"

Mrs. Jackson snorted, amused. Her Mr. Jackson was intelligent indeed, but he knew little about the common man. "What if those nice large cobblestones are worth ever so much more than gravel?"

Mr. Jackson slowly nodded. "You think someone pried out the stones to sell?"

"I do. And who better to look the other way than our Head Valet?"

"Which means another set of suspects, should he have threatened to speak of it." Mr. Jackson downed his coffee and rose. "This is too dangerous a matter for us to investigate. I believe we should make an appointment with the sergeant."

12

M r. Jackson felt surprised to be told they might visit the sergeant at their convenience. So he and his wife dressed, left their dog with her minders, and took a taxi to the police station.

Mr. Jackson walked in to find a flurry of activity. Men wheeled carts full of folders and mail. Uniformed officers sat typing reports, while another uniformed group brought in a few rough-looking men in handcuffs, moving them quickly past.

He took his wife's arm, leading her to the main desk. "Hector Jackson for Sergeant Nestor, please."

The man checked a clipboard, then gestured to the right. "That way."

The sergeant rose when they entered, offering his hand. "What can I do for you?"

"My wife has learned something which you may find of interest."

"Oh?"

His wife said, "Our dead valet was looking the other way as men sold the cobbles in that alleyway and replaced them with gravel. I'm not sure which group was involved, but that's more your domain."

"I see. And where did you learn this?"

His wife bristled, probably at the man's tone.

Mr. Jackson stepped in. "You know we can't reveal our sources, sir. But it involves an eyewitness who wishes to remain anonymous."

The sergeant nodded slowly. "And this witness believes ... what?"

Mrs. Jackson said, "She implied that your Mob was involved."

Sergeant Nestor gave out an amused "Heh." Then he leaned his elbows on the desk. "There are a half-dozen such groups out there, Mrs. Jackson, and dozens more petty gangs who might think up such a scheme. But I'll have my men ask around." He leaned back, hand to his chin. "If Mr. Vincenzo tried to blackmail them ..."

They'd not hesitate to destroy those who opposed them. "I thought it best to bring this to you."

"As was wise." The sergeant rose, so Mr. Jackson and his wife did too. "Thanks. I'll look into it."

Mr. Jackson felt curious. "Were you able to speak with the men waiting for Mr. Vincenzo?"

"I did," the sergeant said. Then he looked at Mrs. Jackson. "Carlo relayed your discussion to me. You were right about one thing: the man hated gravel. He'd never go that way. They were waiting for him on the platform there by the back steps."

Mr. Jackson watched his wife as she slowly nodded, eyes narrowing. "So he had some vital reason to go down the alley," his wife said. "He was lured there, or intended to meet someone. It had to be something recent, a change of plan."

Sergeant Nestor shrugged. "If so, no one's talking. The valets swear that, other than him leaving, they never saw a thing. The men assigned to that truck went on vacation the day prior. They'd saved up for years, three weeks time off each. We're still tracking them down."

"That's convenient," Mrs. Jackson said, and the way she said it almost made Mr. Jackson laugh.

"Indeed," the sergeant said. "But we have clear evidence of where the two men went: train tickets, reservations. They took their families: the children were taken from sports, the wives hired housekeepers." He paused, hands clasped on the desk in front of him, glancing aside, then back. "They aren't acting like felons fleeing some impulsive act. Either this murder was very well-planned — and from all accounts, these two aren't highly intellectual men —"

Mrs. Jackson snorted, evidently amused.

Mr. Jackson said, "Or they weren't involved at all."

The sergeant shook his head. "We should know the truth soon enough."

"Oh, that reminds me." His wife fished about in her handbag. "I managed to get a list of the men whose wives Mr. Vincenzo had been ..."

The sergeant looked amused. "I see."

"And I would add a Mr. Clifton Strait to your inquiries. He's the Hotel's Headwaiter. Mr. Vincenzo's death put him at an advantage in certain personal dealings."

The sergeant's face didn't change. "What dealings?"

"The matter's complex, sir, and involves a personal item told to me in confidence. But at least ensure this man has an alibi."

Sergeant Nestor's eyes narrowed. "You know it's a crime to withhold evidence."

Mr. Jackson leaned forward, yet he kept his tone even. "Are you threatening my wife, sir?"

His wife raised a hand. "I wish to find this man as much as you do. I have no real proof of any wrongdoing, only a suspicion. And it's a delicate matter, one which I might be within my rights not to have mentioned at all. I'm only sharing it in order to help."

Uncertainty crossed Sergeant Nestor's face then.

"All you must know," Mrs. Jackson said, "is that the man could have motive."

The sergeant crossed his arms, leaning back. "Very well. But if I find you're holding out on me, I'll drag you both in."

Mr. Jackson thought the man to be blustering more than anything at this point. But he did wonder what the Headwaiter was involved with and how his wife had learned of it!

Mrs. Jackson said, "One more thing: Mrs. Vincenzo had concerns about her father. He hated the man and had threatened to kill him."

The sergeant let out a snort. "Not hard to see why." He leaned both hands on his desk. "Well, you can let Mrs. Vincenzo know her father's not a suspect. He was at a charity event when the crime happened."

Mr. Jackson felt astonished. "However did you learn this so quickly?"

Sergeant Nestor grinned. "My boys were assigned to the event."

This seemed most curious. "Aren't you a homicide detective?"

"Sure I am. But three of my sons stand guard at events. I went by to bring one of them something and saw the man." He let out a short laugh. "You've been around as long as I have, you get to know the big shots."

Mrs. Jackson nodded. "Was there anything else I should ask? When I talk to the wife?"

Sergeant Nestor squinted at her a bit, his lips pursing. "He'd been gone for a while. But the really interesting thing about her is that she wasn't the one who reported him missing."

13

After speaking with Sergeant Nestor, the couple returned to the Hotel and collected Bessie.

But Mrs. Jackson didn't want to wait — she left Bessie with Mr. Jackson and took a taxi to visit Mrs. Vincenzo once more.

On returning to Mrs. Vincenzo's mansion, Mrs. Jackson found a number of fine automobiles parked out front. Just then, a great number of persons — including Mr. Carlo — emerged. If Mr. Carlo noticed her, he didn't acknowledge it.

She waited until the entryway was clear to announce herself to the butler.

After being left standing on the step for a while, the butler returned. "Mrs. Vincenzo is with her attorney at present, but bids you wait in her parlor."

"I'd be happy to."

As she'd not been invited to sit, Mrs. Jackson amused herself by looking around at the photographs. Some were of older people, with and without Mrs. Vincenzo. A photo of a large group of the workers at the Hotel, taken in what looked like a park, sat framed on the mantel. It was a rather informal photo: Mr. Vincenzo had his arms around the shoulders of both Mr. Montgomery Carlo and Miss Effie Raymond.

After perhaps ten minutes, Mrs. Vincenzo appeared, rushing over. "What news?"

"I've confirmed that your father's not a suspect."

The woman sagged; Mrs. Jackson grabbed hold of an arm as she helped her to a seat. She took the chair beside her. "Just rest there. All will be well."

Mrs. Vincenzo covered her face with her hands. "One bit of good news in all this horror." She leaned back, eyes closed as if exhausted. "That was the will being read. Out loud, in front of all those men." She opened her eyes, and tears lay in them. "My husband left three thousand dollars to some girl up north."

Mrs. Jackson gasped. Three thousand dollars?

"The humiliation of it! I feel as though he's killed me instead of dying."

Men had been killed for less. "I know you don't want to speak of this, but I must ask. What's her name?"

"Miss Mary Bluff."

"And you have no idea who this woman is?"

"None." She gazed off into the distance. "That must have been who he meant."

"I beg your pardon?"

She sighed. "He left a note."

What?

"I didn't tell the police. I'm sorry. But his car, his clothes, and his luggage were gone. He said he couldn't stand to be apart from her any longer."

"Where is it?"

"I threw it in the fire. But then Monte wouldn't believe Earl ran off. And when they found him dead —"

"It no longer seemed important."

Her words turned bitter. "Three thousand dollars. I hope the hussy chokes on it."

One more thing for Sergeant Nestor to look into. "I'm so sorry."

Mrs. Vincenzo smiled, patting Mrs. Jackson's hand. "I'll manage." She let out a sigh. "This place was always too big for me. But he seemed so proud of it that I never wanted to say so. I think I'll sell and move to the seaside." She sat straighter, her cheeks gaining their color. "Yes, I think a change would do me some good."

***

When Mrs. Jackson returned, her suite was empty.

She telephoned the police station. It took a while to be connected with Sergeant Nestor, but he seemed fascinated with what she had to say. "Three thousand dollars? That's quite a motive! Did she happen to say where the woman lived?"

"Just up north somewhere. But I'm sure her lawyer must know."

"Right," Sergeant Nestor said. "Thanks."

After Mrs. Jackson hung up the phone, she heard Mr. Jackson and Bessie come in through the parlor door. "I'm in here," she called out, then went to meet them.

But Mr. Jackson did **not** appear happy. "How could you possibly think that George or his father would be responsible for the Head Valet's death?"

Mrs. Jackson felt entirely confused. "Wait. What happened?"

"I took Bessie for a walk around the block and George was standing out back on the platform. Smoking! I asked why in the world he would start smoking. He said he heard it calmed the nerves. I had to drag it out of him that you'd been asking about his father."

"I asked about his father, yes. But I never accused either one of them of anything. I learned from Mrs. Vincenzo the first time I spoke to her that he'd been there in the weeks before her husband's death, so at dominoes I inquired as to what his father did for a living. He asked if I suspected his father and I told him no."

Silence fell between them.

"This isn't like him," Mr. Jackson finally said. "If he lied to me about this, then he must feel he can't share the truth of whatever troubles him."

For a man as open and honest as her Mr. Jackson was, this must be distressing. "Then you mustn't press him on it any further. He'll speak of it when he's ready."

He seemed disgruntled. "I suppose." Then his face brightened. "Want to have lunch now?"

She grinned, taking his arm. "I would indeed."

On the elevator, Mr. Jackson said, "Would you like to see Miss Denton's show tonight?"

This sounded exciting. "I'd love to!"

The elevator doors opened and they started down the hall. "Very good. We're meeting George in the lobby at seven; we can have dinner there."

It sounded as if the matter had already been arranged. "And what if I'd said no?"

Mr. Jackson shrugged. "Then we'd go another time." He stopped there in the hallway, taking her hand. "I don't mean to intrude upon your life. I just want to make you happy."

She smiled to herself at his words. "I'd be glad to go with you. But we'd better call Mr. Raymond and Mrs. Knight to make sure they can be there early."

He smiled at her fondly. "Already done."

The dining room was as packed full as ever. While they were finishing their meals, the dowager Duchess approached. "Did you enjoy the games last evening?"

Mrs. Jackson smiled at her. "We did!"

"What are you doing after lunch?"

The couple looked at each other, then back at her. "We have nothing planned," Mr. Jackson said.

"Would you like to visit the library?"

"That sounds good," Mr. Jackson said. The couple rose, following the dowager Duchess out to the lobby.

"That reminds me," Mrs. Jackson said, "I haven't returned the books I checked out the last time."

"How did you find the one I showed you?"

"*Walden*? Pretentious, boring, and in some parts, offensive. I didn't finish it."

"I'm sorry to hear that," Duchess Cordelia said. "It's said to be a classic work."

Mr. Jackson laughed. "Let's return this 'classic work' and find you something more suitable."

The three turned towards the grand fountain to cross the wide lobby, but in came Sergeant Nestor and two of his men, all dressed for the street. The sergeant strode straight towards them.

"Good day, sir," Mr. Jackson said.

The sergeant said, "Who gave you that list?"

Out of the corner of her eye, she saw Mr. Jackson glance towards the dowager. "Why do you ask?"

But went straight past them to Duchess Cordelia. "I ought to arrest you right now."

"Sergeant Nestor," Mr. Jackson said, "may I ask what's wrong?"

"You may," he replied. "Did you happen to read that list before you gave it to me?"

The couple glanced at each other. "Sorry to say," Mrs. Jackson said, with some chagrin, "I didn't."

"Well, the last entry was Mr. Flannery Davis."

Mr. Jackson frowned. "The Hotel's manager?"

"Yes. And not only was Mr. Davis undergoing minor surgery at the time of the incident, his wife was horrified at the accusation that she'd been entangled with his Hotel's Head Valet." He turned to Duchess Cordelia. "How could you make such a claim? Interfere with someone's marriage like that? Not to mention waste the time of this investigation?"

Duchess Cordelia's eyes reddened, her lip quivering. "My poor Albert would be here today, comfortable and well, if not for that man's bullying. Do you not think my marriage has been interfered with? My time wasted? My life beset by accusation? All because Mr. Flannery Davis felt compelled to make my husband's life a misery. Well, now Mr. Davis knows how it feels."

Sergeant Nestor, for once, had nothing to say.

The dowager thrust her hands out, head turned away. "Put me in a cell if you must."

"My Lady, I don't think that'll be necessary. But the next time you want revenge, think of who else it might harm. I believe you owe Mrs. Davis an apology."

Duchess Cordelia's face fell. "I do regret that. I never meant harm upon her." She glanced at the couple, embarrassment on her face. "I'm sorry to involve you in this. I'll go wait in the library."

Mrs. Jackson felt embarrassed as well. What must this sergeant think? "I'd have never given you the list if I knew any item on it was false."

"Well, the information Mrs. Vincenzo gave you seems to be correct, at any rate," Sergeant Nestor said. "We found Mr. Vincenzo's car."

Mrs. Jackson said, "Where was it?"

"In a tow lot nearby. It'd been picked up around the corner for being parked too long. His luggage was in the back. We're checking everything for fingerprints."

So he did intend to leave, as his wife said, Mrs. Jackson thought. "Mr. Carlo seemed convinced Mr. Vincenzo wouldn't leave the Hotel. But I wonder ... if he meant to leave his wife that day he was murdered, where he planned to go."

14

When Mr. Raymond came to dress Mr. Jackson, he examined the hair under his beard and sighed. "Your rash seems, if anything, worse."

"What could possibly be causing this?"

"I've done all I know." He began carefully combing Mr. Jackson's beard, trimming it as he went. "Just keep with the hot towels before bed. If it doesn't improve in a few days, we might need to consult a doctor."

"It seems a good plan," Mr. Jackson said. "I've been wondering: do you think exercise might help?"

Mr. Raymond considered this. "It certainly couldn't hurt. I know of several fitness clubs nearby. I'll leave a list at the front desk for you."

"Splendid!" He still didn't feel entirely comfortable around the man, but the more he'd gotten to know him, the more he approved. Very professional.

Mr. Raymond brushed off Mr. Jackson's jacket. "There! Have a wonderful evening."

***

Club Patruni certainly looked impressive. A grand marquee, lit all round by electric bulbs of gleaming gold. Past the sidewalk, the entry was tiled in marble.

But they didn't go in that way. Mrs. Jackson let the men lead her to the side entrance, labeled "Private."

The door opened on Mr. Jackson's triple knock.

"We're friends of Carrie," Mr. Jackson said.

The man who opened the door was very well dressed, yet burly. "Yeah?"

Mr. Jackson gave the man a winning, slightly embarrassed smile. "Well, we've only just met."

The man gave him an amused grin. "In you go."

As they followed the man down a long flight of stairs then along a narrow hallway, Mrs. Jackson whispered, "You'd do well on the stage."

She felt pleased to hear Mr. Jackson chuckle in reply.

Another equally well-dressed man stood guard over a second door. The first said, "Front row."

Beyond this second door lay a large hall. Dozens of small round tables, beautifully set, lit by small candles in the center. Waiters moved here and there in the glow of a wide stage an easy step up. Behind it, a jazz orchestra on a platform another easy step up finished a set. The room burst into applause.

The second man spoke into the ear of a third. This man turned to them. "Your hats, sirs?" After George and Mr. Jackson exchanged their fedoras for tickets, the man escorted the three to a front row table.

A waiter came up. "What will you be having?"

Mrs. Jackson said, "Tea for me, thanks."

"Coffee, heavy cream," said Mr. Jackson.

George stared at them. "You're in a speakeasy and not drinking?"

The couple glanced at each other, Mrs. Jackson unsure how much to reveal. Mr. Jackson said lightly, "Neither of us drink alcohol, but feel free to if you wish."

George looked put out. The waiter stood there.

"Gimme a whiskey sour, then," George finally said. "And separate checks, if you please."

"That's entirely unnecessary," Mr. Jackson said once the waiter left. "I invited you."

"I know you invited me. But I pay my own way."

Mr. Jackson shrugged, then leaned close to speak into her ear. "I should've told him we don't drink."

She nodded. "All's well."

A few minutes later their drinks arrived. The music was perfect, the food, delicious. But Mrs. Jackson's real interest was in seeing Ophelia's show.

A heavyset, dark-haired man stepped up on the stage. "And now, the show you've all been waiting for: The Patruni Girls!"

Two rows of women came out wearing high sequined headpieces and gossamer robes, much like the one she'd worn on the yacht. Yet the robes were adorned with sequins and gems, and so were the gowns they wore underneath. The women met in the center then twirled round to all corners of the stage, their robes flying out around them.

The crowd cheered and whistled, and one by one, the women spun, casting their robes just past the edge of the stage to slide off onto the floor. Their sleeveless gowns came to their ankles, glittering golden and red. Now that the robes were off, the sheerness of the gowns showed the scanty undergarments beneath.

The cheers grew ever louder! The ladies began to dance, making elegant circles, moving forward and back in rows, then combining to cross the rows.

Someone nudged her. "Look there," Mr. Jackson said in her ear.

Yes! There in the third row danced Ophelia, wearing so much makeup that at first Mrs. Jackson didn't recognize her.

Now forming one dancing row, the group began to unclasp their gowns, twirling out of them at the right back corner of the stage, then skipping along. These new garments covered what underwear might, yet these were bedazzled with gems and tassels, which danced as much as they did.

The women danced for some time, kicked up as one, then posed in a grand finale.

Mrs. Jackson shouted, "Bravo!" as the crowd roared their approval.

A pair of older women began collecting the scattered garments as the dancers lined out.

Mrs. Jackson turned to the men. "What a show!"

"They certainly don't have anything like that back home," Mr. Jackson said.

George shrugged. "I prefer the acrobatic ones."

"Oh, you," Mrs. Jackson said, feeling playful. "We can go see one of those sometime if we must."

George leaned back with a drink and chuckled.

The heavyset man stepped casually up to the stage and spread his arms wide. "Ladies and gentlemen," he boomed, "the floor is yours!"

The orchestra struck up a new piece, and couples began stepping up to the stage to dance. The man making the announcement stepped down and approached their table. "I heard this was your first time here. How do you like it?"

Mrs. Jackson wondered a bit about the man not introducing himself.

But Mr. Jackson only said, "Splendid!" He rose, extending a hand. "Hector Jackson, sir, at your service."

The man shook it. "Leo Trappola. The proprietor."

George stood. "Nice place you have here."

Of course, she clasped the man's hand as well. But her mind was on other things. She scrutinized Mr. Trappola's face. *This is the father.*

He had the best alibi one might possibly have: the sergeant being there right when the man walked by, just as Mr. Vincenzo was being murdered.

Yet the timing of it seemed curious. Could Mr. Trappola have had Mr. Vincenzo murdered to avenge his daughter?

15

Just then, Ophelia came up, wearing her dark mustard coat, a black sequined headband over sweaty reddish-blonde hair. "You made it!"

Mr. Trappola gave a thin smile, moving on to the next table.

Greetings all round, and Ophelia sat in the empty chair next to Mrs. Jackson. "I have two more shows to do: eleven and one. You're welcome to stay if you like, but it's not necessary."

"Are the shows different?"

Ophelia shrugged. "Yes and no. We have six dance numbers. Sometimes we get new costumes. You'd probably like that part."

"I'd love to see them all." Mrs. Jackson took her hand. "You were magnificent. But we were up late last night. Perhaps a rain check?"

"Of course." Ophelia gave her a warm smile, squeezing her hand. "I'd love for you to see them."

"You both should come by next week," Mrs. Jackson said. "On Monday, when you're both off. We can have tea in our parlor."

George said, "It'll have to be Tuesday: no one gets time off this weekend."

"Oh," Mr. Jackson said. "Labor Day weekend. I'd forgotten."

"That seems unfair," Mrs. Jackson said.

George shrugged.

"Tuesday it is, then," Mr. Jackson said. "Come by after luncheon."

Ophelia said, "That would be ducky!"

Mrs. Jackson smiled fondly at her.

Mr. Jackson said, "How long do you have? Before you have to return?"

Ophelia glanced at Mr. Trappola standing a few tables off, then stretched her legs under the table with a smile. "Until ten-thirty, I'm free as a bird."

"Let's get you some refreshment, then," Mr. Jackson said. He waved a waiter over. "Give the young lady whatever she likes, and put it on our tab."

Mr. Trappola nudged the waiter and spoke in his ear. The waiter leaned over then and said something to Mr. Jackson, whose face lit up in surprise. "How very kind!" He turned to Mr. Trappola and nodded.

While the waiter took Ophelia's order, Mrs. Jackson spoke in Mr. Jackson's ear. "What was all that about?"

Mr. Jackson said quietly, "Apparently Mr. Carlo discovered we were here. He's asked Mr. Trappola to send him the bill for tonight's outing."

"Interesting." It was particularly interesting if Mr. Trappola had murdered Mr. Carlo's cousin. "But fortunate for us."

Mr. Jackson laughed. "Indeed it is."

She watched Mr. Jackson talk and laugh with the others. What would it have been like, to grow up never having a moment's worry about money? Yet it didn't seem to have spoiled and hardened his character, like the over-application of money to children so often did.

She said to Ophelia, "Where's the Ladies' Room?"

Ophelia grabbed her hand. "I'll show you."

Mrs. Jackson told the men, "We'll be right back."

The Ladies' Room was just as fine as the hall: a row of mirrored dressing-seats, the floor tan marble. As Mrs. Jackson put on new lipstick, Ophelia said, "How did you like the show, really?"

"Didn't you hear what I said? I loved it!"

Ophelia shook her head in disbelief. "You're a strange one."

"Whatever do you mean?"

"You talk and act so old-fashioned. Yet when you see me dressed like this," she opened her coat to show off her sequined undergarment-looking outfit, "you don't bat an eye."

Mrs. Jackson let out a laugh, feeling coy. "Well, I suppose I'm not your ordinary woman." Her cheeks heated up as she looked into Ophelia's eyes. "And I think you're beautiful."

Ophelia blushed, wrapping her coat around her. "We best get back before they start looking for us."

The two went back to their table and listened to the music once more. Yet Ophelia seemed to be looking at them more than at the show.

After a time, Ophelia leaned over. "Do you really like me?"

Mrs. Jackson smiled to herself. "I do."

"And you really like him?"

She considered the matter. "I do."

Ophelia seemed a bit pensive after that.

When the music paused, Mr. Jackson said, "I'll send a taxi for you after your work from now on. What time will you be ready?"

Ophelia gaped at him. "Um ... we have to help clean up after. Half past two?"

He smiled broadly. "Half past two it is."

She seemed at a loss for words. "Thanks!" Then she kissed Mrs. Jackson on the cheek, whispering, "I like you too." She waved to the others. "Goodbye!"

Mrs. Jackson felt touched at Ophelia's declaration.

The table rang forth with farewells, then George called for the check. Yet he seemed dismayed at the total. "Did I really have that many drinks?"

He **had** drunk quite a few ...

Mr. Jackson said, "Just have them combine checks."

George's face darkened. "I won't do that."

Mrs. Jackson leaned forward. She realized he didn't know the situation. "But —"

"No," George said, "and that's final."

Mr. Jackson said, "Can I spot you the difference?"

"I suppose," George said, clearly disgruntled.

Mr. Jackson got out his wallet and handed over a fiver. "That enough?"

"More than," George said. He waved over the waiter and paid the bill.

When he made to hand back the change, Mr. Jackson waved him off. "You might need that. Just pay me back when you can."

George crossed his arms and looked away.

"Well, then," Mr. Jackson said, "shall we be off?"

George said nothing on the cab ride home.

The couple got out at the Hotel. George did say goodbye, at least. "It was a lovely evening."

"See you tomorrow," they called out, and returned to their suite.

"I'm sorry about George," Mr. Jackson said. "I think he's had too much to drink."

Mrs. Jackson nodded. Clearly something was bothering him. But she figured that whatever it was, he'd talk about it sooner or later.

"I have a surprise for you," Mr. Jackson said. He brought out a box. Inside were her shoes, good as new!

"Oh, thank you." She threw her arms around his neck. "They look perfect!"

***

That night, Mr. Jackson lay thinking about how such small things as fixing a pair of shoes brightened his wife's day.

But this gave him an idea. This young Chef had known his wife. Perhaps he might be able to speak with her, see how she was really faring. He might even have some idea as to how best to help her.

The next morning, he woke early, well before breakfast, excited about his idea. "Come on, Bessie." Clipping on her leash, he headed down to the kitchen.

After allowing Bessie to do her business outside, Mr. Jackson stood by the back entry to the kitchen, which was well down the hall from the door to the docks.

The kitchen seemed to be busy, yet not frantic. The aroma of freshly-brewed coffee filled the air. A few were slicing fruit and chopping vegetables, but most of the staff there were placing cloths and silverware rolled up in napkins upon rows of meal carts.

To Mr. Jackson's surprise, George came up, taking off his apron.

George seemed just as surprised to see him. "What are you doing here?"

"I could say the same of you."

George let out a laugh. "The Headwaiter telephoned late last night: wanted me to cover breakfast instead of dinner this week."

"Well, that's good, I suppose." Then he remembered why he'd ventured here. "Might I speak with your Monsieur for a moment?"

"Let me check."

All this time, Bessie had been sniffing the area, and right as George was leaving, she let out a sneeze.

George glanced back. "Bless you!"

Her ears went up, tail wagging.

Mr. Jackson scooped Bessie into his arms. "I hope you haven't caught a cold."

Leaning against the entryway, he pondered this. Did dogs get colds?

Perhaps he should keep an eye on her.

George returned. "Follow me."

Still carrying Bessie, Mr. Jackson followed George past rows of sparkling marble counters, a maid counting napkins, and several others sorting clean silverware.

In the very back, an office door stood open. A large chalkboard hung beside it upon the wall with the day's menu written upon it.

Mr. Jackson peeked around the threshold. The office was small, with cabinets and shelves everywhere.

In the midst of this, the Monsieur sat at a desk writing into a ledger, a stack of papers beside it. He glanced up, surprise on his face. "Please, sit down!"

Mr. Jackson turned to George. "Thanks!" Then Mr. Jackson sat, resting Bessie on his lap. He said to the Chef, "I hope I'm not disturbing you."

The young Monsieur set his pen down, leaned back, hands behind his head, and smiled. "I could use a break." Then he leaned forward. "How may I help?"

How to begin? "I'm sure you know as well as anyone the trials my wife has faced."

The Chef shrugged. "Only a few. She seemed well when last I saw her, before leaving for Paris. We hadn't seen each other for a few years until the other day."

Mr. Jackson felt dismayed.

"Would you like me to speak with her?"

"If you might. I know it's not been very long since her calamity. But she's grieving, and I honestly don't know how to help."

Monsieur rested his elbows upon his desk, hands bridging in front of his chin. "What exactly happened there? Do you know?"

"Only what it said in the papers. She's not spoken a word about it."

Hesitation crossed his face. "I was in Paris at the time. I heard nothing until the police contacted me, just before the Hotel did."

"The police?"

"Yes, well, from their interviews, they learned my connection with him." He let out a breath. "I don't believe I was a serious suspect, being in Paris the entire time, yet I can see why they might think I could be involved." But then he shook his head. "But even if I wished to harm the man, I wouldn't. Revenge is bitter from beginning to end, leaving nothing for the future."

"Forgive me, sir." This man was a decade younger. Yet Mr. Jackson had never up to then felt so unsure. What could he say? What should he say? "What I know for fact is that she witnessed her husband's murder, becoming injured during the battle. I found her at the station and persuaded her to let me accompany her." Recalling her surprise at seeing him by the ticket counter amused him even now. "That's all I know."

He blinked, confusion upon his face. "And ... you're truly married?"

Mr. Jackson nodded. "It seemed the best way to protect her." He pictured the happiness in her smile. "It's only been a few months, but I think it's worked well."

"I wish I had more for you. Perhaps my parents —"

Mr. Jackson raised a hand to stop him. "Please, sir, no. If word got out that we were here, it would put her into danger."

The Chef blinked. "Of course, but —"

"I trust you to be discreet because my wife does. But I don't know these others."

The young Monsieur nodded quickly. "I understand. I'll not speak of her to anyone."

Relief washed over him: they were still safe here.

"I leave for the local markets at four-thirty; have her give a note to the Headwaiter the night before if she'd like to accompany me. Or if that's too early, she can meet me at the roof gardens. I'm usually there by seven: I like to watch the sun rise."

Mr. Jackson thought she'd never want to get up that early in either case, but he said, "I'll let her know."

The Chef smiled to himself. "Or if that's still too early, this time of day would work well." He glanced aside. "The nice part of being Head Chef is that much of the preparation is done by others." Then he chuckled, looking down at the open ledger before him. "The bad part is paperwork."

Mr. Jackson grinned. "I'll leave you to it, then. Thank you, sir."

***

As a peace offering to Sergeant Nestor, Mrs. Jackson volunteered to call the names on Duchess Cordelia's list.

It was tedious but necessary work, taking several days. During this time, her Mr. Jackson had suddenly decided to take up sport. He'd gone to several fitness clubs to tour the premises and interview the proprietors.

She wasn't sure why he might not just have his men do that, but it seemed to make him happy. When he returned each time, Bessie would do her usual sniffing about the entire suite then flop into her little bed, eyes shut. He, on the other hand, returned invigorated, full of ideas about topics from their next trip to what he and George might do on the man's next days off.

Mrs. Jackson loved to see her Mr. Jackson beaming with enthusiasm each day. And he seemed genuinely concerned for her well-being. How am I so fortunate, she thought, to have found such a partner in life?

It presented such a contrast: none of the men on Duchess Cordelia's list seemed happy. Most were angry at both their wives and Mr. Vincenzo, some expressing relief or even gladness at his death. All but three, however, had alibis for their whereabouts.

Sergeant Nestor came to call the morning of Labor Day, dressed more casually than ever before.

"I don't suppose you police get the day off?"

He chuckled. "Actually, at my level, I do. I was on my way to a barbecue."

When she presented the many pages of notes to him, he actually appeared impressed, as well as sobered. "I've misjudged you: this is excellent work."

She felt amused at his admission. "We've both wanted the same thing all along: to solve this crime, each for our own reasons."

This brought a suspicious gleam to his eye. "What are your reasons for doing this?"

For an instant, this took her aback. "I suppose I enjoy puzzles," she finally said. "I find the entire matter most curious. And your shelter and care of us here has been more than enough payment."

She regretted saying that last sentence as soon as the words came forth: he'd be reminded of how they got into this camaraderie.

It seemed the Feds still wished to question her about her first husband's murder. She wasn't sure what story her Mr. Jackson had given the last time they'd stayed here, but Sergeant Nestor and Mr. Carlo had helped hide her. In exchange, of course, for the couple's assistance in solving several deaths right here in the Hotel.

After the terrible night she'd fled her city, she'd had many reasons to hide. She was the only living witness to what had happened. If the men associated with those who killed her husband searched for her out in the wide world, then those she cared about back home might remain safe, or at the very least, alive.

They'd be watched, for certain, in case she might try to make contact. But eventually, those men would grow tired of watching, tired of searching for her. So the longer she stayed away, the safer the people she loved would be.

And as long as men like Mr. Carlo, Sergeant Nestor, Mr. Jackson, and his men continued to protect her, she'd be safe here as well.

Sergeant Nestor laughed. "Never fear, Mrs. Jackson, I have no wish to bring myself under any further scrutiny than I must. You'll not be called as witness to any of it."

"I'm relieved," she said. "As I'm sure your budget office will be."

He grinned. "I do believe you're right."

***

The next afternoon was warm, yet high storm-clouds gathered. The sun peeked out from time to time, bathing the room with light.

Mr and Mrs. Jackson, George and Ophelia sat round the rosewood table in the parlor sipping lemonade.

Mrs. Jackson thought the parlor quite lovely, with its black, cobalt, rosewood, and brass decor. Along with the perfect shade of white upon the walls, the room seemed quite airy.

The clock on the parlor mantle struck three. They'd been chatting for some time, yet George seemed moody, unusually quiet.

Mr. Jackson stirred, bringing out a smallish black velvet box. "In honor of George's birthday," he said, handing the box to him.

At first, George appeared taken aback. He opened the box, and in it was the gold watch her Mr. Jackson had been admiring at the gift shop.

George got very still, then his face turned angry. He set the box down.

Mr. Jackson said, "What's the matter?"

George stood, pushing back his chair. "If I wanted to be some rich man's pet, I'd have stayed home with my father!" He left the box on the table, closing the door to the hallway more forcefully than needed.

Ophelia said, "What was that all about?"

Mrs. Jackson had no idea.

Mr. Jackson sat, mouth open, then it looked as if he'd come to some insight. "Pardon me," he said, then left as well.

Ophelia leaned over with a wry grin. "Never fear: I'll be your pet anytime."

This made Mrs. Jackson laugh. She patted Ophelia's hand. "Then my Pet you shall be!" Although she felt sure Ophelia must be joking, she hastened to say, "Mr. Jackson's a kind and generous man of great wealth. I, on the other hand, have very little to my name." Everything she'd built had been lost when she fled her past life. "I'm quite grateful for his regard."

Ophelia chuckled. "How else might it be, even for such a modern woman as you?"

"I thought you said I was old-fashioned."

"We all have to change sometime." Ophelia leaned back, lemonade in hand. "You strike me as someone who's made many a change in your day."

Had she? "The biggest one, of course, was coming here." She leaned towards Ophelia upon an elbow, chin upon her hand. "But perhaps my second was inviting you to luncheon."

"Oh," Ophelia said. Then she smiled as if she'd made quite the achievement. "Then I'm grateful I happened to notice you following me." But then the young woman sobered. "I hope George is well. He seems a decent sort."

Mrs. Jackson nodded. "I think he is."

Ophelia said, "Do you really like my show?"

"I thought it was lovely." Why keep asking this? "The real question is do you like performing it it?"

"I do. But when Mr. Jackson asked about my mother, I ... I wonder if she'd approve."

"You told me she'd want you to be happy."

Ophelia gazed at the floor, nodding slowly. "I think she would."

"Of course she would. Are you happy there?"

"I do. But I miss spending time with you."

Mrs. Jackson felt moved. "I miss spending time with you as well. We should go holiday shopping."

"I'm not sure who I might shop for," Ophelia said. "But I'll make myself a list."

"We can do whatever you like."

Ophelia smiled, her cheeks coloring. Then she glanced at the clock, and her face turned alarmed. "I need to go. My friend's out of town, and I promised I'd look in on her mother. I'd best hurry if I'm to be back home in time for dinner."

Mrs. Jackson rose, kissing Ophelia's cheek. "Then you should go. Have a wonderful afternoon."

***

It didn't take long for Mr. Jackson to catch up to George: he stood leaning against the railing on the platform outside the kitchens, head down.

The noises of the dock must have made it so George didn't hear him approach, because he jumped a bit when Mr. Jackson leaned upon the railing beside him. He spoke sharply. "What do you want?"

"I just want to know what's going on."

"Well, I'd like to know the same thing."

"What do you mean?"

"Do you get your kicks off of rescuing puppies?"

Thinking of Bessie, Mr. Jackson let out a laugh. "I don't know what you mean."

"You clean up after me on the boat, you pay for my dinner, you get me this much too expensive watch. You 'spot me' an entire week's pay. You want me to go on this huge trip with you. Do you buy all your friends?"

"What? No!" Mr. Jackson felt dismayed. "It's not like that at all."

George turned to stare out over the parking lot. "My father told me since I was small to be my own man. Now he demands I return home and take over the business. Well, I won't be handed my lot in life. And I won't be beholden to him, you, or anyone else."

Mr. Jackson couldn't believe what he was hearing. "Beholden?" For an instant, he had no idea what to say.

"Your wife saved my life earlier this year, and for that I'm grateful. But I'm not a child. And I won't be owned by anyone."

He moved away, and Mr. Jackson grabbed his arm. "George, wait."

George shook off his grasp, hard. "What." His face said: *I can't fight you or I'll lose my job.* His stance said: *But I will if I have to.*

Eugene stood in the parking lot at the bottom of the left set of stairs. "You boys all right up there?"

George glared at him. "Yeah."

Eugene looked to Mr. Jackson, who nodded.

Then Mr. Jackson turned to George. "Please don't do this." How might he say it? "I never meant to make you feel this way." In spite of how awful he felt, he blurted out, "I guess I'm just a generous guy."

Whether it was what he said or how he said it, a laugh burst from George. He returned to the railing. "Too generous, by half." Then he said, "I could never wear that watch. I'd be looking over my shoulder all the time."

Mr. Jackson smiled to himself. "Then let's get one you like better."

***

Mrs. Jackson felt glad when both men returned to the suite. From their faces, it seemed that George and Mr. Jackson had resolved their differences.

And since the men were off to purchase a watch, Mrs. Jackson decided to see what she might learn about the mysterious truck.

She brought Bessie to the lobby level then turned left, then right down the hall to the veterinarian's. One of his boys was on duty, a lad of perhaps fifteen. "Might you watch Bessie for an hour?"

The boy beamed. "I'd be happy to!"

Returning to the main hallway, Mrs. Jackson recalled what Mr. Jackson had said the last time they'd stayed here about the layout of this place. She turned right, walking past the windows displaying the gardens, then turned left.

The smell of food and the noise of trucks increased as she went until she reached the intersection her Mr. Jackson had told her about. To the left was the kitchen, to the right, an elevator and the door to the platform she'd seen from the street.

She went through the door to stand upon the balcony there. Far across the parking lot, a truck stood parked. Other trucks had backed up to the loading dock to her right. A truck emerged from the underground dock to her left, then went up the driveway.

"Can I help you?"

With a start, she turned to face the man who'd been at the dominoes game. "Yes ... Eugene, am I right?"

His name was right on his coveralls.

He grinned. "I remember you, Mrs. Jackson."

She gave the truck parked across the way a quick glance. "Have the police done with that yet?"

"I believe so."

No one stood guard. "Might I look at it?"

"Be happy to escort you."

Mrs. Jackson followed Eugene down the stairs on the left and across the lot to the truck. It had no doors, room for two up front, and a flat area in back with wooden sides.

She didn't approach the truck, just peered at it. It looked new. "What kind of truck is this?"

"Model TT. Pricey, but good at hauling heavy stuff."

"You know a lot about it."

Eugene let out a short laugh. "I better: I'm the one who's gonna fix it when it breaks."

The back area was empty except some gravel in the corners. "What kind of men drive this one?"

"They keep to themselves, don't complain." He shrugged. "Not much to say."

She moved to the passenger side and leaned into the cab. The foot rest was curved, going to a padded bench seat. If anything small were dropped, it'd get wedged ...

A reddish glint caught her eye. "You have a knife?"

"Sure." Eugene fished out a pocketknife and opened it for her. "See something?"

"I do." Dusting off the floorboard, she sat upon it and carefully worked the tip of Eugene's knife under the glinting area.

A small red gemstone.

Heart pounding, she folded the knife and handed it back to Eugene.

The gemstone sat on the floorboard, murky red.

Was Mr. Jackson's valet involved in Mr. Vincenzo's murder?

"You okay, Mrs. Jackson?"

Was Mr. Jackson in danger?

16

S he picked up the gem and put it into the zippered area of her handbag. "I'm fine." She stood, dusted herself off. "Let's look at the tires."

The tires had gravel stuck in them. Eugene shook his head in distaste. "They were supposed to clean this out before they left for vacation."

"Were they now."

"Yeah. I've never seen them leave a truck like this."

"That's very interesting."

Eugene stood there a moment. "You think someone drove this without permission?"

Mrs. Jackson nodded. "It's very likely." Equally likely was that these men gave the keys to whoever drove it.

The two returned to the platform. "Thanks so much for letting me look at it," Mrs. Jackson said. "This has been very helpful."

Eugene tipped his cap. "Glad to be of service."

"And say hello to your wife for me, will you?"

He beamed, cheeks coloring. "I surely will."

She smiled as she watched him bounce down the steps. *Men in love are all the same*, someone told her once. And it was true.

Mrs. Jackson retrieved Bessie and returned to their suite. When she got to her rooms, Mr. Jackson hadn't returned, but it wasn't yet time for tea. Bessie began her usual sniffing of every inch of the suite.

Mr. Jackson didn't like for her to smoke in their rooms, so Mrs. Jackson stood out on the balcony instead.

She loved looking out over the water. Being out on the open water these past few months had cured much of what ailed her. Helped her begin to grieve.

And the thought that Mr. Jackson might now be in danger terrified her. It was as if her worst nightmare had come to pass.

Why was that gemstone in the truck? And what did it mean?

Mr. Jackson had told her his valet knew the two men who drove the truck. During a ride, or even just sitting in the truck, he could have lost the gem.

The valet could have borrowed the truck for some quite innocent reason and lost the gem then.

Or Mr. Stanley Raymond could be Mr. Vincenzo's murderer.

The man didn't look like a murderer. While he seemed to dislike Mr. Vincenzo, many people did — including her Mr. Jackson. And Mr. Raymond didn't look strong enough to move a manhole cover it'd taken three men to pry out.

Besides, Bessie liked him.

Whether this valet of his was involved with Mr. Vincenzo's murder or not, she couldn't tell Mr. Jackson what she'd discovered.

She knew him well enough to know he wasn't the kind of man who could hide his true feelings. He'd act differently. If Mr. Raymond was innocent, it'd surely offend him. If he were guilty, it'd tip the man off and he'd flee.

So she had to learn the truth herself, and soon.

She put out the cigarette and went to the phone. "The police, please, non-emergency line."

It took a while to get Sergeant Nestor on the line. "What can I do for you, Mrs. Jackson?"

"I just learned something which may interest you. The two men who drove the truck were supposed to clean the truck entirely before they left on vacation, down to prying the gravel from the tires. One of his coworkers said that they'd never left a truck in this condition before."

"Well, that's interesting. Explains the fingerprints."

"Oh?"

"Let's just say that they're not those of our drivers."

"So you did find the men."

"Yeah, and you won't believe what they're saying."

"What's that?"

"They think they're being set up."

"Well, that **is** interesting. Are they saying by who?"

"No, they won't say. I'm not sure they know. But we know where they are now, and I have local officers watching them."

Mrs. Jackson considered telling Sergeant Nestor about the gem. But even if they might prove the gem belonged to Mr. Raymond, it only showed he was in the truck before they arrived here. So the gem proved nothing. She needed more.

***

While Mrs. Jackson pondered the true meaning of the gemstone, Mr. Jackson was taking George Neuberg out to buy a watch.

When they entered the watch store, the proprietor hurried behind the counter to greet them. "Welcome, good sirs. Did you have something special in mind?"

George took off his old, beaten-up watch. "I'd like to replace this in a similar style."

"I have a selection of leather-strap watches right here." He went around behind the U-shaped glass counter to the far left, sliding open the glass. He lifted a long display board, resting it to stand upon the counter.

Mr. Jackson thought privately that they all looked much the same, but after some consideration, George chose one along with some leather oil for the strap.

George stretched his arm out to admire his new purchase. "This is just what I wanted."

"My pleasure," Mr. Jackson said, and the two shook hands. "Happy birthday."

Leaving the old tattered watch with the proprietor, they went to a bistro nearby, taking one of the small tables near the window. The waiter came up. "What can I get for you, sirs?"

"Tea and toast," George said. "And separate checks, if you please."

"Coffee for me, heavy cream." Mr. Jackson felt amused. If the man wanted to pay his own way, he'd certainly allow him to.

And after the waiter had left, George lowered his voice. "I didn't know you don't drink."

Mr. Jackson shrugged. "Never cared for it. And my wife came to grief over it long before we were married."

George's eyes widened. "Sorry to hear that."

The obvious question hung in the air. "I don't believe she minds if you drink in front of her, but you'd have to ask."

The waiter set their orders down, along with their checks, then moved on.

Mr. Jackson poured his cream, then took a sip. Not bad. "I've been thinking about what you said that day upon the platform." How might he say this? "My situation is unlikely to change. I daresay, I hope it never does. Yet I realize it puts you in a dilemma."

George snorted quietly.

"As it turns out, my wife's quite the modern woman." He smiled to himself, a surge of fondness coming over him. "And she very much looks forward to you joining us when we travel."

Instead of answering, George spread jam upon his toast and took a bite.

He'd felt shocked when George told him how little he made for all the work he did. "Have you enjoyed being a waiter?"

George considered this as he chewed, swallowed. "It sounds strange to say it, but I do. Yet I see the need for improvement in the way the front house is run."

Mr. Jackson nodded. "What things might you do?"

As George began outlining his plans for improving the Hotel's restaurant service, Mr. Jackson watched him. And he saw his error.

He'd wanted to smooth the way for the younger man, offer experiences that George might never get on his own. Yet for George, the adventure lay in overcoming the obstacles to his personal success.

"So what do you think?" George took up his teacup and over the edge of it, their eyes met.

He loved the way George's cheeks colored. "I think I owe you an apology."

George set the cup down.

"But we can't be pals if you're going to lie to me."

George's face fell. Then he nodded.

"There we have it." Mr. Jackson smiled, feeling relieved. "I've decided to join a fitness club. I get a free pass each month. Want to join me next week for tennis?"

"I've never played."

Mr. Jackson fancied himself quite accomplished at it. "You taught me dominoes: it's only fitting that I return the favor."

***

Mrs. Jackson felt relieved when Mr. Jackson returned safely to their rooms. "How was your trip?"

He seemed more relaxed than she'd seen him in some time. "Quite productive, I'd say."

She went to him, putting her arms around his waist. "Let's stay in for dinner."

He smiled at her. "I'd love to. Just let me call down to let them know we won't need Mr. Raymond or Mrs. Knight this evening."

She'd forgotten that they were assigned through the front desk. This was perfect. If Mr. Raymond inquired, the desk clerk could say he spoke with Mr. Jackson and all was well.

"Have them send up the evening news as well," she heard Mr. Jackson say.

She kicked off her shoes, stretching out upon a chair. "Oh, before you hang up — have them give me a wakeup call for six."

He did so, then put down the receiver. "You're meeting with *le Monsieur Chef* tomorrow, then."

She smiled at him. "Indeed I am."

It wasn't that she hadn't wanted to meet with the Chef up to now, but each day, the work with Duchess Cordelia's list had left her fatigued. Now that it was completed, and she'd had a chance to recover, she felt intrigued to see what the young man had to say to her.

Duchess Cordelia had been subdued for the past days since her embarrassment, almost quiet. At first, the old woman's rage at her husband's fate felt startling, but as Mrs. Jackson considered the matter, she'd come to understand. She'd made certain to reassure the dowager that things were still well between them.

Mr. Jackson sat beside her. "Why so pensive?"

"Just thinking of Duchess Cordelia. You know, every one of the names on that list was true, but —"

"Sergeant Nestor will only remember the false one."

"Yes. I feel bad for her, though I know I shouldn't."

"She's dependent on the Hotel. It must be a difficult way to live, having been in such wealth as she was."

Mrs. Jackson sighed. That was the way of it for women — always dependent on someone to survive.

"Something's wrong."

She considered the matter. "Do you think it wise to withhold information when it might be harmful?"

Mr. Jackson shrugged. "To a child, certainly."

His meaning was plain: adults had the right to be told. What should she do?

He knelt before her, took her hands. "My dear girl, I'm not a child. Whatever this information is, it can't harm me. And I'm not going anywhere. Remember what I promised? If you ever decided you'd rather be free, I'd release you at once. Though if you said that," he took a deep breath and let it out, eyes moist, "I'd truly mourn."

"It's not that." She rested her hand on his soft scratchy black beard. "I fear for you."

Surprised, he drew back. "For me? Why?"

At present, she was out of new ideas. And he was ever so good at them. So she told him about the truck and the gem.

Mr. Jackson sat on the floor tailor-seat for a full minute in silence. Then he leaned back, hands behind him, and looked up at her. "You feared he'd learn of what you found through my reactions."

She nodded.

"Thus staying in for dinner."

She grinned, chuckling, yet tears welled up. She tried one answer then another, yet none seemed suitable.

"Come here." he said, and she sat on the floor beside him. He wrapped his arms around her; she rested her head on his chest. "You're probably right. I'm not nearly as good as hiding things as you are. But I'm grateful I've never had to." He kissed the top of her head. "Whether this man has done something wrong or not, I'm sorry now that I kept Mr. Raymond on. I've not felt comfortable with him. And instead of acting to secure a different man that very first day, I continued in spite of it. And now we're in a pickle."

"Don't say that. I won't have you blame yourself."

"But I do, for the main reason that now you're in tears on my account." He turned to face her, taking her hands. "I am not going anywhere, I promise. I have no plans to die, and if for some reason I dropped dead this instant, it wouldn't be because of anything you've done. Please stop fearing for our future."

It'd been so long since she dared to believe she had a future that she began to cry.

He kissed her hands, then leaned his elbows upon his knees, her knuckles upon his forehead. Then his head rose, and he kissed her hands again, his eyes red. "We'll get through this," he whispered, a wry smile on his face, "whether you believe me or not."

The absurdity of the whole thing made her laugh. All over a gemstone! "We shouldn't dismiss the man. But until we learn the truth, he mustn't come here."

Mr. Jackson nodded, his face sober. Then he rose. "I'm tired of sitting on the floor."

She laughed. They sat around the table to wait for their dinner to arrive.

"I'll learn the truth," Mrs. Jackson said, wiping her eyes. "Surely someone must know one way or the other what went on that day."

"That the police haven't already questioned?"

"Eugene said the truck's drivers would never have left it in the state it's in. Less than a day went between the time the men left and the killer took the truck. So assuming the men really did clean the truck before leaving on vacation, the fingerprints on it have to be those of the killer."

"That would be reasonable."

"So how did the killers get the keys? Sergeant Nestor says the men believe they've been set up, but don't know by who."

"Interesting. So it's reasonable to assume these men didn't give the keys to anyone."

"Not if they're innocent. And Sergeant Nestor says the fingerprints don't match those of the men."

Mr. Jackson rocked backwards a bit, blinking. "The killers stole the keys."

"And I can't imagine the keys were left for anyone to take. They must be under lock themselves. So unless these killers are also master lock-pickers, they left a trace of their crime." She nodded to herself. "Eugene would know if anything was broken." She glanced at the clock. "He's gone home for the day, but I can speak with him tomorrow."

The parlor bell rang, and Mr. Jackson rose. "That would be our dinner."

She smiled up at him. "I'm glad we stayed in now."

***

The next morning, Mrs. Jackson and Bessie emerged from the elevator onto the roof as the sun peeked over the horizon. The Chef stood dressed in dark blue facing the sun, his hands behind his back.

Peace radiated from him, so different from the bitter, angry young man he'd been.

She moved toward him; he turned to her and smiled. "I hoped you'd visit."

A large garden stretched before them, planted in large, decorative boxes, raised to knee high and carved with intricate patterns. Many stood free, yet many were covered in cloth. Some plants she could identify, others left her baffled. Yet each was beautifully tended and lushly growing. "You come here every day?"

"Indeed I do." He gestured out over the plants. "The best way to eat is food you tend yourself." A thin smile touched his lips. "The garden had been sadly neglected when I arrived. But it's recovered somewhat, with a bit of love."

Mrs. Jackson felt surprised, sure that the dowager's husband — who loved gardens — would have tended it.

Had he been gone that long? All that happened seemed like yesterday. "And you went to the market at half past four?"

He smiled fondly. "I did. You see, I've been rising at four since I was a boy. The kitchens don't tend themselves." The Chef stretched out his hand to her. "Come, there's much to do."

According to him, they'd had unseasonably hot weather up to now, but a freeze was predicted. "If the tomatoes are left out tonight, they'll spoil, and the plants will die. We must gather every one and bring the plants inside for the winter."

So she let Bessie roam around the large outdoor swimming pool — now covered — and sniff the various area of the roof. In the meantime, they went among the boxes, removing the cloth, gathering tomatoes into large trays upon wheeled carts as they went. For a time, she got lost in the work, focused on collecting each of the round little fruits.

"Your husband has been concerned for you," the Chef said.

She smiled to herself. "I gathered."

A silence fell as they moved the full carts over to the elevators and selected empty ones, then returned to collect the remaining tomatoes. Far below, a distant hum of traffic, the chirp of a bird, Bessie's soft noises as she went here and there, the opening of the elevator door, the sound of feet.

His voice broke the quiet. "I don't wish to presume."

Bessie came and sat nearby. Men wheeled large barrels out, and began to dig out the bare tomato plants, setting them gently into the barrels, dirt and all. After they'd placed several into one barrel, they'd bring out another. She felt fascinated by their work, yet she turned to the Chef. "Say what you wish, sir."

His face fell. "I don't mean to offend. Yet ... if any harm has come to my life, it was in the bottled-up secrets of others exploding into vengeance. And I've learned it can cause more harm, even if the secret be hurtful, to keep sorrow hidden rather than share it with those who love you."

For some reason, this made Mrs. Jackson blush.

The young Chef seemed not to notice. "Your husband seems a good man. But if you can't speak to him about your sorrows — and they don't involve him — find someone you can speak with. Anyone will do." He placed the last tomato into the cart, dusted his hands off and laid his hand upon her shoulder. "Don't let what happened then destroy your life now."

They wheeled the last cart over, then the Chef took up a large basket. It was then she noticed the short black apron he wore. Retrieving a knife and a pair of gloves from the apron, he handed her the basket. Then they moved past a long box full of cabbages to another grown thickly with foot-tall leafy plants. He began working quickly, cutting the plants off at the base and putting them into the basket she held.

"What's this called?"

"Endive. Freezing will damage it as well. Tonight, I'll include it in a salad and an appetizer. Whatever remains will be soup tomorrow."

"That's very wise."

"The Hotel is lush and expensive and grand," he cut off a plant and put it into the basket, "but it's also a business." He moved to the next plant, cut it off. "We have to use every bit we have if we're to prosper in the future."

"You really care about the Hotel."

He seemed taken aback. "Why come here then attach my name and reputation to it if I didn't?"

She hadn't thought of it that way before. "Then the situation with the Head Valet must trouble you."

He dropped the plant into the basket. "I've heard nothing of it. What happened?"

"He was murdered just outside the Hotel."

His jaw dropped, eyes widening. "How horrible! Do they know who did it?"

She shook her head. A whole long line of people had gone along hating the man for years. What could have possibly caused the men who murdered Mr. Vincenzo to do so now?

17

Mrs. Jackson and Bessie returned to her suite to find Mr. Jackson fast asleep. After calling down their breakfast order, she asked the desk clerk to notify Mr. Raymond and Mrs. Knight they wouldn't be needed this morning. Then she sat at the table near the lovely balcony in his bedroom, watching his dear sleeping face.

And her mind drifted to the conversation she'd just had. There was so much she didn't know, it seemed, about the young man who now stood as Head Chef here. Yet she felt pleased at how he'd turned out.

Mr. Jackson had worried for her. Her heart clenched at the thought. *He cares for me.* The thought brought a certain anxiety. Although he'd assured her time and time again that they were safe here, the thought that he might be taken from her ... somehow ... hadn't left her.

Being so early, she didn't expect their tray for at least an hour yet. So she had a leisurely read of the thick morning newspaper, Bessie nestled beside her.

She'd asked for the tray to be delivered to her bedroom so as not to wake him. But when she returned from answering the door, Bessie following behind, he smiled up at her.

"I thought I'd let you sleep a bit." She sat on the edge of the bed beside him and kissed his forehead.

He wrapped his arm round her. "Something smells wonderful."

"Are you hungry?"

His face turned playful. "Ravenous." He pulled her close, pretending to gnaw her ear.

It tickled. "Well, then, I better make sure you're properly fed!" She went to the other room, rolling the cart over by the table. Mr. Jackson had put on his robe, and stood by watching. She lifted the lid.

"Oooo," he said. "Bacon."

She put the plates on the table. Besides the bacon, there was an omelet, crisply roasted cherry tomatoes with herbs scattered atop them, hashed and browned potatoes, and toast.

A carafe of orange juice, another one with water in it, a coffeepot, and a teapot stood on the shelf underneath. All the trimmings of a proper breakfast sat beside them, with a small plate of chipped beef and a narrow bone set aside for Bessie. "My, this is magnificent." She felt touched that they remembered her little dog.

Mr. Jackson helped her set up the table, then set to his meal with a good appetite.

The food was delicious, every bite. She gazed over at him fondly. "Thank you for being concerned for me."

He took a sip of his coffee. "So you did speak with the Chef this morning."

"I did. The view from the rooftop is lovely. And the garden! He let me help in it."

"Oh?"

"I picked those tomatoes!" She felt rather pleased with herself.

He smiled fondly at her. "I'm glad you enjoyed it."

She considered the entire morning. "I did! I don't normally rise so early. But ... I believe I will again." It'd been so peaceful up there.

And she realized this was what she wanted: peace, and some real work to do that meant something.

For some reason this feeling of peace made her think of Ophelia. She felt at home with her. Like they'd been friends forever, and instead of learning each other new, were just picking up where they left off.

Bessie put her paws up on Mrs. Jackson's legs, and she nestled the little dog on her lap. "Sorry to tell you: it's supposed to freeze tonight."

"A pity," he said. "I guess more sailing this year's out of the question."

"I didn't consider that. George's parents will be heartbroken."

"I imagine they'll invite us over sometime during the holidays."

"I hope so. And we can leave Bessie here with people she doesn't feel compelled to bark at."

He laughed.

"How's your neck?"

"Whatever Mr. Raymond's been doing must be working: it's better today."

She didn't know why, but the news gave her a great sense of relief. "I'll feel terrible if he's truly done nothing wrong. It's horrible to suspect someone."

Mr. Jackson nodded. "This may sound strange." He touched his neck. "Yet I felt better at once when you said we'd not have him here again."

The thought of a man who might murder someone with a straight razor to her Mr. Jackson's neck made her shudder. "This is maddening. I must learn the truth. I don't believe I'll rest until I do."

He smiled at her, opening up his the morning news. "Go speak with Eugene, then. Bessie and I will hold down the fort."

But first there was something she wanted to do.

She found the Chef standing out on the platform in back, gazing out over the parking lot and the trees beyond. He twitched when she stepped up beside him. "I didn't hear you!"

"It's noisy out here, isn't it?"

"I admit to being a bit caught up in my thoughts," he said. "How may I help you?"

"I wanted to thank you for speaking with me this morning. I enjoyed it very much."

He smiled. "I did, too."

"Have you seen Eugene? The maintenance man."

"Sorry, I don't know many of the names here."

"I'm sure he'll be by soon." She stood with the young Chef, listening to the sounds of the trucks and men. "There's something you should know."

He nodded soberly.

"You and my former husband may have had your differences, but from the moment I learned of his relation to you, I looked on you as family."

He took a deep breath, in and out. "I seem to have found my family wherever I went. Each cared for me as they could, then let me make my way as I might."

"That's very charitable of you, all things considered."

He laughed. "How many have people all over the world who love them? I hardly consider anymore the few who felt glad to see my back." He checked his watch. "I best return to work — I'm sure they have a whole line of plates for me to check."

She grinned at him. "Enjoy your morning."

"I will."

Right then, Eugene passed by down below, and she waved to him. He jogged his way up the steps. "What can I do for you?"

"I'm curious about the trucks. Do you secure the keys here in any way, or can anyone access them?"

He leaned upon the railing. "Now, that's an interesting question."

"Why do you say so?"

"Because a week before you returned here, someone broke the lock to the key rack. It must have been after all the drivers picked up their keys in the morning."

"Why do you say that?"

"I only learned about it because the man who locks up at the end of the day came to me worried about his truck. The key rack being broke open like that and all. None of the keys were missing, so after I fixed the lock, I forgot all about it."

She considered the matter. "And no one saw who did it?"

Eugene shook his head. "I don't know why that darn fool Davis let those two drivers take three weeks off this time of year. Between the Head Valet walking off in the middle of his shift, a truck out of commission and the tourist rush, we've been so busy a crowd could have carried the truck off without anyone seeing it."

And in the three weeks in between, any fingerprints on the key rack would be long gone. "Thanks, this has been really helpful."

"You think someone here killed Mr. Earl?"

She sighed. "It's looking more like that every day." And just in case Eugene took it on himself to talk about it, she added, "But we still don't have enough to pin it on anyone."

He shrugged. "I just work here."

After speaking with Eugene, Mrs. Jackson returned to her suite.

Mr. Jackson was in knickers and an undershirt doing calisthenics in his room as Bessie ran back and forth around him.

She laughed. "What a sight you two make!"

He straightened, a grin upon his face. "I'm glad we provide you with some entertainment."

"What's spurred on this interest in exercise?"

He took up a towel which lay upon the bed and wiped his brow. "I thought that perhaps it was time for me to begin paying more attention to my health."

"That seems wise; carry on." She went to her bedroom to call for lunch to be delivered to their suite. It came about the time Mr. Jackson emerged from his bath. "Shall I have this set up in your room or the parlor?"

Mr. Jackson's voice emerged from his rooms. "In here is fine."

To Mrs. Jackson's delight, a spicy endive and tomato salad accompanied the meal. "This smells delicious!"

"It does," Mr. Jackson said. "One thing about exercise — it does improve the appetite."

Mrs. Jackson set up a plate on the floor for Bessie, and returned to her lunch, which was delicious.

The couple ate, and talked, and eventually a waiter came and took their plates away.

Bessie, who'd been lying upon the carpet the entire time, suddenly ran off into Mr. Jackson's bathroom.

He turned his head to follow. "I wonder what she wants in there?"

A few moments later, a strange noise came from Mr. Jackson's bathroom. He got up and went there. "Oh, dear. She's gotten sick!"

Mrs. Jackson found him wiping the floor with a damp towel. Bessie lay close by, head on her paws. "Poor little thing."

He rinsed out the washcloth and wiped the floor again. "She probably ate too much."

Bessie didn't look right. "I don't know ... she's never done this before. Stay here: I'm taking her down to have the vet look at her." She scooped the little dog up in a clean towel and headed out of the door.

The veterinarian took a quick look at her. "You're right: she doesn't look well. Let me do some tests and keep her overnight. Has she eaten anything unusual?"

"We just feed her off of our plates."

"But no chocolate or fruit?"

"We haven't had any chocolate for a while, to be honest. And I didn't know a dog would eat fruit."

He laughed. "Dogs will try to eat just about anything." His wife brought over a padded kennel box, and he gently placed Bessie into it. She lay there, eyes shut. "This is easier to clean should she be sick again."

Mrs. Jackson smoothed little Bessie's hair. "I'll be back to see you tomorrow."

Bessie opened an eye, and her ears went up a moment, but then she rested again.

Mrs. Jackson went to the lobby and out front, feeling discouraged. Would Bessie be okay?

And what were they going to do about Mr. Jackson's valet? How long might they keep avoiding him before he felt something was wrong? She felt no closer to understanding how the man was involved with this than when she discovered the gem the day before.

Perhaps she should have told Sergeant Nestor about the gemstone.

Mrs. Jackson lit a cigarette. The day was pleasant at any rate, the air crisp. The holidays were coming soon. What might she get for her Mr. Jackson?

"Waiting for a taxi, ma'am?"

A blond valet she'd seen earlier but not met before stood nearby. She shook her head. "Busy today?"

His nametag said: Charlie. "Not yet."

Something had been bothering her this whole time. "May I ask you something?"

The man seemed surprised. "Why, certainly."

"My husband and I are helping Mr. Carlo about the matter with Mr. Vincenzo."

He nodded gravely.

"Were you here that day?"

"Yes, ma'am, I was. I already told the police about it, though."

"Told them what?"

He glanced over towards the alley. "One minute he was there, the next he's gone."

"Just like that?"

"Yeah."

"Why do you think he went in the alley?"

Charlie blinked several times, mouth open. "Wait."

"What is it?"

"I forgot. Right before that, one of the maids came out and talked to him. She went right back in, so I guess it slipped my mind."

This interested her at once. "Which maid was it?"

He squinted, eyes unfocused. "I'm kinda new here ... not sure if I heard the name right. Essie?"

"Effie?"

"Yeah, that's it. Effie. Pretty girl, that one. But Mr. Earl'd get mad if you so much as looked at her."

Mrs. Jackson dropped her cigarette and stepped on it. "And did he say or do anything after that?"

Charlie shrugged. "Kind of seemed annoyed, tell you the truth. He headed over there," he pointed at the alley, "but then a car came up, so I quit looking."

"I see."

"Do you think it means anything?"

"I think you've been very helpful."

Mrs. Jackson rushed to the front desk, where the young man who'd greeted them at their first arrival back here stood. "Might I use your telephone?"

"Certainly!" He placed it upon the counter.

She dialed the police station. "Sergeant Nestor, please."

It took a while for him to answer. "What can I help with, Mrs. Jackson?"

She spoke quietly. "I know who killed Mr. Vincenzo, and I'm almost certain why. But we must hurry if this is to be done without a scene. Come to our suite after tea. But quietly, and bring a few men with you. No uniforms, and not a word to Mr. Carlo."

Sergeant Nestor sounded amused. "Be right over."

When she next caught the eye of the desk clerk, she said, "Might I speak with Maria, please?"

"She should be in her office. I'll call her out here."

He took the phone, speaking quietly into it while Mrs. Jackson watched the grand fountain. A few minutes later, footsteps approached her.

It was Maria, the Head Maid.

"Ah, there you are," Mrs. Jackson said. "Would you send Effie to my room after tea? I'm going to need her help for a few hours."

"Certainly," Maria said, making a notation upon a pad. "I'll let the front desk know where she'll be."

"Perfect! Thank you so much. And tell her not to bring her cart — it won't be necessary."

Mrs. Jackson hurried to her suite, finding Mr. Jackson in the parlor reading a book.

When he saw her, he closed the book and set it aside. "How's Bessie?"

This distracted her, just a bit. "What? Oh, yes. They're going to watch her overnight." She had to focus. "This is important. Is Mr. Raymond coming to dress you this evening?"

Mr. Jackson put down his paper. "I haven't called to tell him not to." He hesitated, then his mouth fell open, his face horrified. "No."

She nodded. "Yes, sorry to say. Sergeant Nestor will be here after tea."

Mr. Jackson put his face in his hands.

She sat beside him, moved. He'd trusted the man, and to get confirmation of his crime must feel like a blow. "I'm sorry. That new blond valet saw his sister speak with Mr. Vincenzo right before he went to the alley. But I just can't see her knowingly sending the man to his death."

"So someone sent her there to speak with him."

"And drove that truck. And killed him."

His eyes widened, but he quickly recovered. "You called the sergeant ... so I presume you have a plan?"

She sat beside him. "We have a few hours before he arrives. Here's what I think we should do ..."

18

When the knock came at Mr. Jackson's door, Mrs. Jackson answered. "Oh, hello, come in. Mr. Jackson is delayed." She turned round, heart pounding, relieved when the man followed. "Would you care for some tea?"

"No thank you, ma'am," Mr. Raymond said. He closed the door behind him.

She continued on into the parlor. "Feel free to sit here until he arrives."

"That's very kind of you." Yet although he came into the room, he continued to stand, glancing about.

Mrs. Jackson said, "Oh, that reminds me! I found something of yours." She went to her handbag and fished out the red gem.

When she showed it to him, he looked astonished. "Wherever did you find it?"

Mrs. Jackson smiled. "You see, that's the problem. If you consider all the places you've been, that is."

The man paled. "What do you want?"

"Nothing. But I'm curious as to why you did it."

His face grew guarded. "I don't know what you're talking about."

Mrs. Jackson slipped the gem into her pocket, then rested a hand upon the back of an armchair. "Let me see if I can figure it out. You break the lock in the key rack when no one's looking and steal the truck. You lure Mr. Vincenzo to the alley with your sister's help. Then you drive up in the truck and bring out the shovels and crowbars. Once there, he helps you dig out the manhole leading to the sewers and hoist it up. You have him look down into there, and while he's doing that, you give him a good whack on the head."

A gasp came from her room.

Mr. Raymond jerked towards the sound, face alarmed. "Who's there?"

The doors opened from all three sides and policemen came in, dressed for the street. Mr. Jackson came in from his room.

Sergeant Nestor entered from Mrs. Jackson's room. Along with the sergeant was Effie Raymond. "Stanley," Effie said, "what have you done?"

"You can't prove a thing," said he.

Sergeant Nestor appeared entirely relaxed. "Oh, but we can. You see, from talking to your coworkers at the Howell-Green Procurement Agency, I learned something interesting: you never wear gloves. From the truck drivers' coworkers I learned another interesting thing: those men were meticulous about their truck. They did a thorough clean-down before leaving for their vacation, inside and out. All the men did their clean-outs at the end of the day, so I have several witnesses to it.

"And what do we find on the truck now? Fingerprints, upon the steering wheel, the door-handles, two crowbars, a large stick ..." he seemed to be at a loss.

Mr. Jackson exclaimed, "So that's what you used to mark the manhole!"

Sergeant Nestor nodded, his face suggesting he'd not considered that. "And upon one of the shovels, which although you tried wiping it down, also had Mr. Vincenzo's blood type upon it. I'll be willing to wager that when we go to the station, those fingerprints will be yours. His fingerprints lie upon the other. Mrs. Jackson has given an excellent rundown of the crime. The question we all have is: why?"

Mr. Raymond crossed his arms.

Effie looked heartbroken. "He told me why. When we argued. When I spilled the soap, right before you two arrived. He said, 'Effie, I can never forgive what he did.'"

Mr. Raymond took a step forward. "Don't tell them about that! After all you've been through?"

Mrs. Jackson had a theory as to what this might be about. "Effie, dear, tell us what happened. No one else need know."

Effie glanced around at the men filling the room, then hung her head. "I thought Earl loved me. He said he'd leave his wife. But then when I came with child, he told me he'd talked to Mr. Carlo about it. He never could leave: his wife would cause a scandal." She let out a sigh. "So I went up north and had my girl there."

Ah, Mrs. Jackson thought. "Mary Bluff?"

Effie stared at her, mouth open. "How did you know? I named her after my mother!"

"Your Mr. Vincenzo left her three thousand dollars in his will."

Effie's eyes filled with tears. " I knew he cared about her." She fished in a pocket for a handkerchief. "She's with good folk. I send money every month." Effie began to cry. "I thought it'd be too hard to come back. But the work's better here. And I still loved him, even after all he's done." Then her face twisted in anguish. "He was her father." She turned on her brother. "I'll **never** forgive you for this!"

Mrs. Jackson felt a great sadness. The man wanted to be with his only child.

Mr. Jackson said, "I agree it's a difficult situation. But enough to kill a man over?"

Mr. Raymond flinched, then his face reddened, fists balling up.

Mr. Jackson glanced at Effie. "Would he not help?"

Effie sniffled, wiped her nose. "No, Earl's paid for everything." She raised her eyes to her brother. "Stanley, what's this really about? What did he do to you?"

Mr. Raymond's hands began to shake, and he stumbled backwards, face white.

Alarmed, Effie lunged forward. "Stanley!"

She and one of the policemen rushed to the valet's side, helping him to a chair.

"I feel ill." Mr. Raymond put his face into his hands, looking very young somehow. "I don't even know where to begin. It all seems too horrible to relate."

Sergeant Nestor pulled up a chair and sat across from him, then drew out a pad and pencil. "Just start where you feel best, son."

Mr. Raymond nodded, hands still covering his face. "I was seven. Effie was only four, so she probably don't recall it. But my parents had a terrible fight. I remember Papa saying, 'You betrayed me with **him**?'. At the time, I didn't understand, but when Papa stormed out, I followed. I wanted to be with him. I don't think he knew

I was behind." His hands dropped to his lap, and he began panting as if he'd just run a mile.

Sergeant Nestor nodded. "Go on."

"Papa went to this building and up two flights. They were long flights. Straight, made of white stone. I didn't go up the second one. I stayed on the landing. It was dark, but I felt scared to let Papa see me there. At the top there was a light and a door. Papa banged on the door. The man answered. They argued, fought." He squeezed his eyes shut. "He pushed my Papa down the stairs!"

Effie gasped.

His hands began to shake. "I saw that man's face up there lit by the lamps as clear as day."

Mr. Jackson looked horrified. "Earl Vincenzo."

Mr. Raymond glanced back at him, then nodded. "It was. I didn't know he'd been seeing Effie until she brought him by, before she came with child." His jaw tightened. "My Papa dying like that killed Mama. But at her grave I promised I'd make Vincenzo pay for what he'd done. Come to find out he'd hurt dozens of women. And then, when he cast my sister aside too, I couldn't stand by no longer."

Effie blurted out, "He thought you were his friend!"

"Then my plan worked."

Sergeant Nestor said, "How did you get him to go to the alley?"

Mr. Raymond smiled to himself. "While Effie was up north, I learned where he worked and went by once in a while. Then I sent letters telling him I knew he'd killed a man. Eventually he let his distress show, and I offered my help. When the two truck-men said they were going on vacation, I made my plan. Told him I'd caught the man who'd been sending the letters and stashed him. I'd bring him close by to meet up and have words. I'd have Effie tell him where and when."

"So that was the message," Mr. Jackson said.

Effie turned pale. "I told him Stanley said he'd meet him in the alley."

Mrs. Jackson nodded. "That new valet Charlie said he seemed annoyed."

Effie's head drooped. "He was. Earl said, 'Now?' And I said, 'Yes, Stanley's waiting for you!'" Tears ran down her face. "I persuaded him to go!"

Mrs. Jackson said to Mr. Raymond, "But how could you have possibly known the manhole cover was there?"

He laughed. "We grew up right behind the Hotel. Used to play in that alley with my friends. I'd seen the manhole many a time, back when there were cobbles. Didn't take but a few minutes with a stick to find it again and mark the spot."

Sergeant Nestor turned to Effie, face stern. "You knew your brother asked you to send Mr. Vincenzo to the alley. And then he turned up dead there. Why didn't you come forward?"

"And doom my brother?" She put her face in her hands. Then she raised her tear-streaked face. "I suspected. When we argued it was because I asked if he had anything to do with Earl gone missing. But when I knew he'd killed him, I didn't know what to do!"

Mr. Jackson said, "Is Mr. Vienna really delayed?"

Mr. Raymond shook his head. "I doubt he knows you're back. I'd been hanging round the operators and happened to catch the call when the one on duty took her break. It seemed miraculous. I figured after the other murders a few months back, you'd be called in. And being your valet I'd know if you got suspicious." His tone turned ironic. "Guess you fooled me."

Sergeant Nestor put his pad and pencil away. "Come along now, lad, it's time to go. Let's not make a scene."

"What'll happen to Effie?"

"She had good reason to suspect you and didn't come forward. I'll have to charge her, but who knows? The judge might be lenient in this case."

Mrs. Jackson said, "May I speak with Effie for a moment?"

Sergeant Nestor took Mr. Raymond's arm and led him to the door. The other men nodded, moving away.

Effie turned to Mrs. Jackson. "I'm so sorry for everything."

She looked so young, so forlorn. Mrs. Jackson put her hands upon Effie's upper arms and spoke quietly. "Look at me. You have nothing to be sorry for. I know what it's like to try your best to do what's right and still lose everything. I just wanted to say something a friend told me recently: don't let what happened then destroy your life now. Whatever happens, someday this will be over. And when it is, go somewhere no one's ever heard of you and live your life. You still deserve it."

Effie hugged her, weeping. "I will, ma'am. I will."

Mrs. Jackson hugged the girl back, feeling maybe the whole ordeal she'd been through had given her something after all.

Once everyone left, Mr. Jackson put his arm around her waist. "Was this the secret of Effie's that you couldn't tell me?"

She smiled, yet she didn't feel it. "It was." Then she turned to him. "I have no secrets from you." Then she sighed. "I know you want to know what happened to me that night we left, because you care. It's just ..."

"It's too soon to speak of it."

And, as Mr. Raymond had said, it seemed too horrible to relate. She nodded.

He gave her a warm smile and kissed her forehead. "Let's go out for dinner."

So they did.

Epilogue

Mr. Stanley Raymond was convicted of the premeditated murder of Mr. Earl Vincenzo and sent to prison.

Miss Effie Raymond was charged with withholding evidence in a homicide investigation and put on probation. She was also dismissed from the Hotel. Under the circumstances, though, the court allowed her to move up north to be with her daughter. The Headwaiter, Mr. Clifton Strait, moved there as well.

Mr. Hector Jackson decided that the couple wouldn't travel any further until George Neuberg had saved up enough to comfortably accompany them, which pleased George no end. In turn, George applied for and was granted the Headwaiter's position, which came with a substantial raise.

Miss Ophelia Denton decided she'd keep her present dancing job, but with reduced hours. She and Mrs. Jackson spent many a pleasant afternoon holiday shopping together.

The dowager Duchess Cordelia Stayman was ever so pleased to receive a box of dominoes from the couple as a gift for her hospitality.

Mr. Norman Vienna resumed work as Mr. Jackson's valet, and was Mr. Jackson glad to see him!

When the couple retrieved Bessie, the veterinarian had a surprise for them. The little dog's escape from her leash on the steamer before the couple arrived at the Hotel had its consequences.

Bessie was expecting puppies!

The next book in the Myriad Mysteries is coming soon!
To learn more about the Myriad Mysteries,
visit Claire Logan's Facebook page.

Acknowledgements
Thanks so much to Tina Crist for her beta reading, and to Patricia Loofbourrow for the cover design.

About the Author
I've loved reading since I can remember! I love puzzles and mysteries and intrigue, and of all the cities I've been to, Chicago is my favorite. My four years living in Chicago during grad school were wonderful. Plus I love history. And wasn't the 1920's wild? I've always wanted to write a fun mystery series set in Chicago and now here's my chance.

Made in the USA
Columbia, SC
21 June 2022

62014244R00105